A DEEPER PART *of* Myself

A Story of My Grandmother
Lillian Burse Adcock Wiggins

CAROL WIGGINS GIGANTE

WestBow Press books may be ordered through booksellers or by contacting:

WestBow Press
A Division of Thomas Nelson & Zondervan
1663 Liberty Drive
Bloomington, IN 47403
www.westbowpress.com
1 (866) 928-1240

ISBN: 978-1-9736-9648-3 (sc)
ISBN: 978-1-9736-9649-0 (hc)
ISBN: 978-1-9736-9650-6 (e)

Library of Congress Control Number: 2020912543

Print information available on the last page.

WestBow Press rev. date: 07/29/2020

After this manner therefore pray ye:

Our Father which art in heaven,

Hallowed be thy name.

Thy kingdom come,

Thy will be done in earth,

as it is in heaven.

Give us this day our daily bread.

And forgive us our debts,

as we forgive our debtors.

And lead us not into temptation,

but deliver us from evil:

For thine is the kingdom,

and the power,

and the glory,

forever. Amen.

Matt. 6:9-13 KJV

My Granny Wiggins died before I was born, so I have spent my lifetime wondering how it might have been to be loved by her, to be taught by her, to share little secrets and snuggle at the end of the day. It just wasn't meant to be. So, I listened and read and researched until I found a most remarkable woman who I am proud to call Granny.

This book is dedicated to all those who knew and loved her, and those who have an ache in their hearts for not having had that privilege. Also, my sister, Jane Moore, who has been a tremendous source of encouragement during this journey.

Lillian Burse Adcock Wiggins

My Granny Wiggins

A beautiful life, overcoming death with the promise of eternal rest but far too soon.

1910

At this stage in her life Lula Fry Adcock had given up on her dream of traveling. During her school years so long ago, she had pored over every geography book her teacher would allow, even some from the higher grades. The crowded classroom held all eight grades of students almost as eager to learn as she was. Lula would always be ready to dash out the classroom door as soon as the last bell rang, but even at school, there were chores to be done. There was water to be carried from the spring for the next day, books to be stacked neatly on the shelves, and always the floor to be swept. The other girls made every effort to include her in their after-school activities and the teacher had even invited her to her own home a few times, but although she was willing to help out around the classroom, her greatest desire was to hurry home and do her own chores, which strangely enough, repeated practically everything she had just helped with, then head over to the tiny library out in the boonies, studying other worlds. Her family marveled at her dedication.

But life has a way of changing course. This life in the hills of Tennessee – Coalfield - to be exact, was all she had ever known and she had convinced herself that it would never be any different. What chance did she have of bettering anything about her life? She had met and married William Adcock seventeen years before in 1893, and in spite of the grief of their baby girl, Martha, being stillborn fourteen years ago, she thought they'd had a good life. The little niggling pain in her heart had lessened over the years and now she was content to

learn what she could as her children studied and pass along her wide range of knowledge to them.

Packing another quart jar with the verdant leaves of the poke salad plant, she smiled to herself. "Lord, I ain't meaning to complain but this taking care of kids and doing all this housework over and over ain't exactly my idea of the good life," but the good Lord seemed to remind her that she had it better than most. People all around her were losing their jobs and their land. Measles and typhoid ran rampant all across the area and you couldn't help but worry about your little ones being taken.

But some women just seem to be born practical. Lula and her sisters, Lena and Margaret, and even the younger ones, Sarah, Mary and Virgie had been taught to plan ahead, while at the same time, making do with what they had. They had spent many nights sitting around the stove in Lula's kitchen, tearing up old sheets and preparing poultices just for such a time as this. They would just keep praying that none of their family be struck down with any of these diseases, but they knew in their hearts that there wasn't much more they could do to prepare. Surely Doc would stay on top of things.

This day, however, Lula didn't have time to worry. But she *was* wishing for an extra hand or two. In her mind she went over each possibility. William had been up until the wee hours of the morning with an ailing cow so he was catching a wink or two in the back room. Her father, Melvin Fry, had moved in with them a few months ago and sincerely thought he was helping around the place, but there were so many of his chores that Lula and William had to do over. The children adored their Papaw Fry, so it was secretly decided that loving and watching out for them would be Papaw Fry's main chore. Evan, their oldest child, being sixteen already, had been trusted to take the mule and work in the log woods for a day or two to make a little extra money. Randolph, age thirteen, and Dewey, eleven, had been sent to the feed

1910

At this stage in her life Lula Fry Adcock had given up on her dream of traveling. During her school years so long ago, she had pored over every geography book her teacher would allow, even some from the higher grades. The crowded classroom held all eight grades of students almost as eager to learn as she was. Lula would always be ready to dash out the classroom door as soon as the last bell rang, but even at school, there were chores to be done. There was water to be carried from the spring for the next day, books to be stacked neatly on the shelves, and always the floor to be swept. The other girls made every effort to include her in their after-school activities and the teacher had even invited her to her own home a few times, but although she was willing to help out around the classroom, her greatest desire was to hurry home and do her own chores, which strangely enough, repeated practically everything she had just helped with, then head over to the tiny library out in the boonies, studying other worlds. Her family marveled at her dedication.

But life has a way of changing course. This life in the hills of Tennessee – Coalfield - to be exact, was all she had ever known and she had convinced herself that it would never be any different. What chance did she have of bettering anything about her life? She had met and married William Adcock seventeen years before in 1893, and in spite of the grief of their baby girl, Martha, being stillborn fourteen years ago, she thought they'd had a good life. The little niggling pain in her heart had lessened over the years and now she was content to

learn what she could as her children studied and pass along her wide range of knowledge to them.

Packing another quart jar with the verdant leaves of the poke salad plant, she smiled to herself. "Lord, I ain't meaning to complain but this taking care of kids and doing all this housework over and over ain't exactly my idea of the good life," but the good Lord seemed to remind her that she had it better than most. People all around her were losing their jobs and their land. Measles and typhoid ran rampant all across the area and you couldn't help but worry about your little ones being taken.

But some women just seem to be born practical. Lula and her sisters, Lena and Margaret, and even the younger ones, Sarah, Mary and Virgie had been taught to plan ahead, while at the same time, making do with what they had. They had spent many nights sitting around the stove in Lula's kitchen, tearing up old sheets and preparing poultices just for such a time as this. They would just keep praying that none of their family be struck down with any of these diseases, but they knew in their hearts that there wasn't much more they could do to prepare. Surely Doc would stay on top of things.

This day, however, Lula didn't have time to worry. But she *was* wishing for an extra hand or two. In her mind she went over each possibility. William had been up until the wee hours of the morning with an ailing cow so he was catching a wink or two in the back room. Her father, Melvin Fry, had moved in with them a few months ago and sincerely thought he was helping around the place, but there were so many of his chores that Lula and William had to do over. The children adored their Papaw Fry, so it was secretly decided that loving and watching out for them would be Papaw Fry's main chore. Evan, their oldest child, being sixteen already, had been trusted to take the mule and work in the log woods for a day or two to make a little extra money. Randolph, age thirteen, and Dewey, eleven, had been sent to the feed

1910

At this stage in her life Lula Fry Adcock had given up on her dream of traveling. During her school years so long ago, she had pored over every geography book her teacher would allow, even some from the higher grades. The crowded classroom held all eight grades of students almost as eager to learn as she was. Lula would always be ready to dash out the classroom door as soon as the last bell rang, but even at school, there were chores to be done. There was water to be carried from the spring for the next day, books to be stacked neatly on the shelves, and always the floor to be swept. The other girls made every effort to include her in their after-school activities and the teacher had even invited her to her own home a few times, but although she was willing to help out around the classroom, her greatest desire was to hurry home and do her own chores, which strangely enough, repeated practically everything she had just helped with, then head over to the tiny library out in the boonies, studying other worlds. Her family marveled at her dedication.

But life has a way of changing course. This life in the hills of Tennessee – Coalfield - to be exact, was all she had ever known and she had convinced herself that it would never be any different. What chance did she have of bettering anything about her life? She had met and married William Adcock seventeen years before in 1893, and in spite of the grief of their baby girl, Martha, being stillborn fourteen years ago, she thought they'd had a good life. The little niggling pain in her heart had lessened over the years and now she was content to

learn what she could as her children studied and pass along her wide range of knowledge to them.

Packing another quart jar with the verdant leaves of the poke salad plant, she smiled to herself. "Lord, I ain't meaning to complain but this taking care of kids and doing all this housework over and over ain't exactly my idea of the good life," but the good Lord seemed to remind her that she had it better than most. People all around her were losing their jobs and their land. Measles and typhoid ran rampant all across the area and you couldn't help but worry about your little ones being taken.

But some women just seem to be born practical. Lula and her sisters, Lena and Margaret, and even the younger ones, Sarah, Mary and Virgie had been taught to plan ahead, while at the same time, making do with what they had. They had spent many nights sitting around the stove in Lula's kitchen, tearing up old sheets and preparing poultices just for such a time as this. They would just keep praying that none of their family be struck down with any of these diseases, but they knew in their hearts that there wasn't much more they could do to prepare. Surely Doc would stay on top of things.

This day, however, Lula didn't have time to worry. But she *was* wishing for an extra hand or two. In her mind she went over each possibility. William had been up until the wee hours of the morning with an ailing cow so he was catching a wink or two in the back room. Her father, Melvin Fry, had moved in with them a few months ago and sincerely thought he was helping around the place, but there were so many of his chores that Lula and William had to do over. The children adored their Papaw Fry, so it was secretly decided that loving and watching out for them would be Papaw Fry's main chore. Evan, their oldest child, being sixteen already, had been trusted to take the mule and work in the log woods for a day or two to make a little extra money. Randolph, age thirteen, and Dewey, eleven, had been sent to the feed

1910

At this stage in her life Lula Fry Adcock had given up on her dream of traveling. During her school years so long ago, she had pored over every geography book her teacher would allow, even some from the higher grades. The crowded classroom held all eight grades of students almost as eager to learn as she was. Lula would always be ready to dash out the classroom door as soon as the last bell rang, but even at school, there were chores to be done. There was water to be carried from the spring for the next day, books to be stacked neatly on the shelves, and always the floor to be swept. The other girls made every effort to include her in their after-school activities and the teacher had even invited her to her own home a few times, but although she was willing to help out around the classroom, her greatest desire was to hurry home and do her own chores, which strangely enough, repeated practically everything she had just helped with, then head over to the tiny library out in the boonies, studying other worlds. Her family marveled at her dedication.

But life has a way of changing course. This life in the hills of Tennessee – Coalfield - to be exact, was all she had ever known and she had convinced herself that it would never be any different. What chance did she have of bettering anything about her life? She had met and married William Adcock seventeen years before in 1893, and in spite of the grief of their baby girl, Martha, being stillborn fourteen years ago, she thought they'd had a good life. The little niggling pain in her heart had lessened over the years and now she was content to

learn what she could as her children studied and pass along her wide range of knowledge to them.

Packing another quart jar with the verdant leaves of the poke salad plant, she smiled to herself. "Lord, I ain't meaning to complain but this taking care of kids and doing all this housework over and over ain't exactly my idea of the good life," but the good Lord seemed to remind her that she had it better than most. People all around her were losing their jobs and their land. Measles and typhoid ran rampant all across the area and you couldn't help but worry about your little ones being taken.

But some women just seem to be born practical. Lula and her sisters, Lena and Margaret, and even the younger ones, Sarah, Mary and Virgie had been taught to plan ahead, while at the same time, making do with what they had. They had spent many nights sitting around the stove in Lula's kitchen, tearing up old sheets and preparing poultices just for such a time as this. They would just keep praying that none of their family be struck down with any of these diseases, but they knew in their hearts that there wasn't much more they could do to prepare. Surely Doc would stay on top of things.

This day, however, Lula didn't have time to worry. But she *was* wishing for an extra hand or two. In her mind she went over each possibility. William had been up until the wee hours of the morning with an ailing cow so he was catching a wink or two in the back room. Her father, Melvin Fry, had moved in with them a few months ago and sincerely thought he was helping around the place, but there were so many of his chores that Lula and William had to do over. The children adored their Papaw Fry, so it was secretly decided that loving and watching out for them would be Papaw Fry's main chore. Evan, their oldest child, being sixteen already, had been trusted to take the mule and work in the log woods for a day or two to make a little extra money. Randolph, age thirteen, and Dewey, eleven, had been sent to the feed

store and would barely be back in time to carry the water and gather firewood before dark. Jennie was only three but insisted on playing with Littie, who, at age four, was hardly more than a baby herself. They were keeping themselves entertained just outside the back door where Lula could keep an eye on them. Vaneda, or Nead, as the little ones had begun to call her, age seven, was on the front steps cracking walnuts for the cake they would make the next day. She was feeling all grown up because her daddy was letting her use his hammer instead of a rock. Lula knew she would have to pick shells out of the nutmeats, but she didn't mind. She would also have to deal with a sore thumb or two.

That just left eight-year-old Lillian in the line-up of helpers. But where was she? Catching a glimpse of her errant daughter skipping across the recently plowed ground that would soon become their garden, Lula stepped to the back door and called to her.

"Lillian B. Adcock, where you been all morning? I needed some help canning this poke salad." Lula wiped the sweat from her brow and watched the girl rinse her dusty feet at the rain barrel, which was actually just a bucket, stop to playfully splash a handful of water in the direction of her sisters, then rush into the kitchen.

Quickly hanging her straw hat on a nail on the wall, Lillian grabbed a dish cloth and began lifting the now-cool jars of greens from the kettle. "I was down at the spring, Mama. Aunt Lena asked me to dig her up one of them big ferns that grows on the bank. She said to do it before the sun got too hot on it."

"My sakes, child, you run around all over like you ain't got no chores at home!"

"I know, Mama, but---" Lillian did feel a little bit of guilt creeping up her spine because she had taken a lot more time than was necessary to dig up and repot the fern. The water, the playful frogs, and the quiet wind sneaking through the trees always beckoned her to "stay a little longer."

"No buts! Now you finish moving them jars out of my way," Lula barked, making a mental note to have Papaw Fry give the girl a haircut in a day or two. The chestnut-colored pigtails had become so ragged on the ends that Lula sometimes thought she must be chewing on them.

"Mama?" Lillian broke the silence after a while. "Do you think Papaw Fry could cut my hair in the next day or two? Teacher says I must be chewing on the ends of my pigtails."

Lula almost dropped the jar she was wiping. Oh, my beautiful daughter! Why would I yearn for other worlds when I have exactly what I want right here? She nodded and smiled as she moved the jar over with the others.

So the two of them worked side by side through the morning, stuffing the jars with the greens, carefully placing them in the boiling water bath then taking them out again when they had cooked enough. Over and over until forty-eight quart jars stood gleaming in the sunlight that peeked through the thin kitchen curtains. They both knew that without their hard work of preserving food, they might go hungry on cold winter days.

Lillian was unusually quiet, making Lula wonder what might be going on in that head of hers. She didn't have long to wait for an answer.

"Mama," the little girl chirped, "when I grow up, I want to be just like you!" Her brown eyes sparkled as she thought ahead to just how it would be.

Even though Lula was pleased, she decided to tease her sweet daughter for a minute. They were always bantering back and forth, with Lula usually getting the last word. "You mean cause I'm so loving and kind?"

"No!" Lillian exclaimed. "I meant 'cause you get to cook and can and clean the house, and work in the garden and stuff and *you've got kids!* I want to be just like you!"

Lula's mouth flew open but she clamped it shut quickly as it dawned on her just how true those words were. She grabbed Lillian in a wrap-around hug. "Thank you, my girl! How did you get to be so smart?"

"Papaw Fry!" Lillian cried, bending double with childish laughter, knowing that her answer would exasperate her mother. She would get the last word this time.

Sometime later, imagining a well-deserved rest, Lillian had barely touched her bottom to a ladder-back chair when Lula called to her. "Come, child. Let's get these to the cellar." Loading their arms with some of the cooled jars, they made their way carefully to the small door at the side of the house – the cellar. Now this was not a favorite place for Lula. At any given time, you might run across a mouse, or even a snake or, at the very least, a spider. But she had learned through the years that no real harm had ever come to anyone there so she sent Lillian in first.

The damp earth felt good to the little girl's bare feet, and since she had never been afraid of the dark, she made an adventure out of it. "I'll go to the back and you hand me the jars," she told her mother.

When they were down to the last four jars, Lula crawled back into the hole. Carefully placing the jars where Lillian could reach them, she suddenly felt something skitter across her foot. Holding her breath to keep from screaming, she heard a faint giggle coming from the back of the cellar. *Snakes don't giggle!* Moving very slowly she made her way back to the door and yelled, "Snake! Lillian come out of there!"

Even though it was her joke in the first place, Lillian came out of the hole faster than greased lightning. "It was a stick, Mama. I had a stick!"

"I'll teach you to scare me, young lady," Lula said, but her own laughter reached Lillian's ears before the words. Round and round the yards they went, ducking under low-hanging tree limbs, crawling under bushes, jumping over a flower bed or two and ending up lickety-split on a grassy knoll beside the barn, thoroughly exhausted.

Papaw Fry leaned on the fence, watching the whole thing. "Couldn't you catch her, Daughter?" he teased, shaking his head. He had lived here with them long enough to know that playfulness was a part of their day. "I think it's time that husband of yours gets busy," he mumbled, and sauntered off toward the house.

Mother and daughter lay on the grass watching the clouds drift lazily across the sky, but it didn't take very many minutes for Lula to rouse herself. "Lillian, get yourself back down to the spring and bring the milk for dinner. All the males in this family tend to be starved right around this time of day."

Lillian jumped to her feet and offered her mother a hand.

"Get on with you, girl. I ain't dead yet!" Lula pushed herself up and headed back to her little world in the house.

Lillian turned and walked the first few steps then broke into a run, heading straight down the hill, back to her most favorite place on earth, the spring. No matter the season, it was a haven for the little girl, a special place where she could open her heart and mind, laying her dreams on the moss-covered rock beside her, then when it was time to go, hiding them under the dark, rotting leaves at the bottom of the pool of water. Who knows what thoughts and ideas were shared with the frogs, snakes, and spiders? Who knows what dreams might have been squelched because it was too hard to battle the kind of life you were dealt? There's a whole wide world out there, Lillian. Sweep away the dead leaves, plumb the depths of that spirit, fly away, fly away!

But for now, the frogs still made her giggle and it was nice to be out of that boiling hot kitchen. Finally, she scrambled to her feet and made it all the way to the top of the steep hill, stopping here and there to gather honeysuckle, ferns, and daisies – Mama never fussed at her when she brought wildflowers and milk. Oh no! The milk – it was still at the bottom of the cold, clear spring!

1912

The children had been good all year but this day they just couldn't resist. Having been taught to come straight home from school every day, not to stop at the store, or stop anywhere to play, and definitely not to wade in the creek, they decided that they would stop and watch the minnows for a few minutes. Surely their mother wouldn't mind just this once because school would be out in another week and they might not get another chance. Just as it is with sin in our lives, one thing led to another and now ten-year-old Lillian, standing on a slippery rock in the middle of the creek, forgot her manners and yelled at her older brother.

"Dewey Adcock, you're nothing but a smart-aleck! You know we weren't supposed to get wet!" She tried desperately to wash the mud from the front of her best school dress. It was the pink one with cherries embroidered on the collar and the creek water was just making the stain worse.

"Sorry, Sis. I was just trying to get past you. These rocks are slippery!" He too was slipping and sliding trying to help nine-year-old Nead across the creek, with Littie, only six but a natural on the rocks, slipping around them and reaching the bank first.

An apology from any of her brothers always melted Lillian's heart and she readily forgave whatever so-called sin they had committed, but this time she would be in trouble with Mama. Today their only concern had been that someone would see them and tattle to Mama; now the worst had happened and her dress was ruined.

It was clearly time to head home so Dewey herded his sisters up the bank to the road where they had left their shoes and socks. Randolph watched it all from the bridge where he had spread his books out to study for his finals the next day. "Boy, are you guys in trouble," he called out playfully, gathering his books and joining them at the end of the bridge. It wasn't long before his well-muscled long legs carried him ahead of them. He patted Dewey on the head as he passed, grinning like a possum eating a sweet potato. "See you at home, fellas!" he called over his shoulder. If they had looked up just then they would have seen him cut across a neighbor's yard and take the shortcut home.

Dewey might have been remorseful at the thought of Lillian's pink dress, but he was still scheming. "Look, Lil, I can sneak you into the house and you can change without Mama seeing you."

Lillian's mouth flew open and she had to use her dress tail to wipe mud from her lower lip. "We can't do that, Dewey – it's dishonest and deceitful and mendaci … mendic … well, anyway, it's wrong!" She sputtered and gave up trying to pronounce 'mendacious' one of her teacher's latest words on her vocabulary list. "We can't do that," she whispered.

Being properly chastised, Dewey changed his tune. "Well, I guess we'll just take our medicine and get it over with."

By the time they reached home they were sick with worry. Would Mama do the deed or send them out to Daddy? They passed Randolph, sitting in the front porch swing, lazily pushing it back and forth with one foot, trying to get back to his studies. He gave them no encouragement. They eased on into the kitchen, not knowing for sure where their mother was. What they didn't know was that someone had already blabbed to Lula about their little excursion so she'd had plenty of time to ponder their punishment.

Dewey, being the oldest of these three, decided he would take the brunt of the punishment. Spotting his little sister, Jennie, playing in the living room, he motioned for her to come. "Sis," he asked, "where's Mama?"

Five-year-old Jennie knew trouble when she saw it and she was in no mood to help. "She told Randolph to watch out for me and she went over to Mrs. Hill's, but she'll be back in two shakes of a lamb's tail," she said, quoting her mother perfectly. She swished her reddish-blond hair back off her face and very saucily informed Lillian that she was hungry.

So they waited. Lillian set out leftover cornbread and poured milk for Nead, Littie, and Jennie. Dewey helped himself then hurried out to the front porch to see if Randolph would like a snack. Refusing with a shake of his head, Randolph continued that slow, back-and-forth motion of the swing, somehow managing to taunt Dewey. I won't let him get under my skin, the younger boy thought as he slung a mighty frown in his big brother's direction and scurried back into the kitchen. He and Lillian finally decided that they should get their homework out of the way, just in case they didn't feel like doing it later. Lillian finished her milk and bread with a quick swallow and went to find scrap paper for Littie and Jennie to play school. Dewey looked over Nead's shoulder while she worked on her arithmetic, their dark brown hair, so much like William's, blending together as one. Then Dewey and Lillian hit the books.

Lula walked into this peaceful scene a few minutes later and began to brag, in a slightly exaggerated manner, about how well her children always obeyed the rules of the house and would never deliberately do anything naughty, like, say, Mrs. Hill's children would, and on and on ... Dewey caught Lillian's eye and muttered, "She knows."

In spite of herself and mostly because she didn't like being compared to Mrs. Hill's kids, Lillian broke into tears and the story came out. Jennie danced around the table singing, "Youn's in trouble! Youn's in trouble!" until Lula sent her outside to play.

So, three days later, in between his usual chores, Dewey was still scrubbing the mud out of Lillian's dress. There were times he had to stop and tend to his blistered knuckles, wondering how come the washboard didn't wear their clothes out completely. Lula had promised that if there was any complaining, she was sure she could find some more dirty laundry, possibly some overalls.

Lillian, Nead and Littie had been directed to the lower end of the garden where, with Randolph's help (after all, he had sat and watched), they were to pull weeds, remove rocks, bust up clods of dirt, and otherwise prepare the ground and plant a "Soup Garden". This garden produce, consisting of tomatoes, onions, peppers, summer squash, and cabbage, would be harvested and passed around to needy folks in the area. All this was William's idea but Papaw Fry, who sometimes cooked for the whole family, was the one who felt sorry for them and volunteered to lend a hand along the way in exchange for a few tomatoes.

Such was the punishment for twenty minutes of after-school pleasure in the creek. Homework and household chores still had to be tended to so there was no spare time for the three girls to play. Jennie proved to be a handful for Lula without Lillian and Nead's capable hands to help, but so be it. Lula and William cherished their children and, as all parents do, looked to the future.

The endless round of school began again that August; garden work being moved to evenings and weekends. The soup garden was deemed a success but not exactly as the adults had originally thought. It turned out that every family in the area had experienced a more abundant harvest than ever before so the family was privileged to donate their produce to the community soup kitchen menu. The hard part would've been the delivery, but that was Randolph and Papaw Fry's job.

And, at long last, it was Jennie's turn to start first grade. She had heard only good things about school from her brothers and sisters, per Lula's orders, so she was beside herself with anticipation, practically skipping all the way out of the holler. ABCs and 123s had come easily for her and you could find her name, perfectly scripted, on various surfaces in and out of the house. Whatever it was that school intended to teach her, she was convinced she already knew that and more.

Within two weeks, the little girl was bored silly, leaving Mrs. Linden, first grade teacher and county nurse, scrambling for ideas to fill her classroom with more exciting learning materials. Thus the pace was set for little girls to dream big and formulate plans to fulfill those dreams.

1916

It took longer for the lot of them to get out of the house these mornings, with the addition of Joe and Gladys into the family. A surprise to them all, the babies had been born almost exactly nine months apart, leaving Lula not only exhausted from all her other chores but running after the two-year-old "almost twins" didn't help any. And it all came at a time when Randolph was caught between being a man or staying a boy for a little while longer. This morning, he chose boy behavior, insisting on pulling the ribbons from Lillian's hair and making her have to start all over with her braids.

"Mama, can't you make Randolph stop? He's going to make us late!" Lillian cried in frustration. Normally she didn't mind his teasing, well, not much, but today she really was in a hurry. *Maybe someday he'll grow up.*

People in the community were surprised that Randolph and Dewey had stayed in school as long as they had when most young boys their age had dropped out long before. Truth be told, they were a little behind their proper grades because of being needed for work occasionally but the teachers were more than willing to help them catch up. Lula had spent time trying to explain that both boys were eager to learn and didn't want to give up the opportunity of a good education. They both were interested in being businessmen some day and wanted to set a good example for the younger children. Lillian listened carefully to these little sermonettes and determined that she too would stay in school as long as possible, even though she knew that several of the girls in her eighth-grade class were anxious to drop out now. Sadly, it was the accepted thing for girls. Housewifely chores and motherhood seemed much more attractive than sitting at a desk for hours at a time, studying subjects that meant nothing to them. Mothers who had failed to pass on such things as cooking, sewing, and child care were now facing the consequences.

It was now February, just barely past the end of the longest semester Lillian could remember, such a long year that the teacher had announced that all eighth graders would be allowed to celebrate that day, and then be dismissed early. Not exactly a party, but there would be a little tribute to Valentine's Day with cookies and punch, so Lillian jumped out of bed early and rushed through her chores.

There were beds to be made, firewood carried in from the back porch, if indeed the boys had hauled it that far, and Lillian suddenly realized it was her turn to fetch water from the bucket they called a rain barrel. She knew it would be frozen over, so she picked up a piece of the firewood to break the ice and slipped out the back door. As warmly as she had dressed it was never enough so she was shivering uncontrollably by the time she was back in the house.

Standing as close as possible to the kitchen stove, she called Jennie over to her and began braiding the child's fly-away hair, anything to hurry them along and make sure she'd get to school on time. She managed to dodge her brothers and their usual harassment and even help with the breakfast of fresh eggs, bacon, biscuits and gravy. Lillian had learned to make gravy years ago just by watching her mother, so now the family depended on her to make it practically every day. Nead had also become quite a baker so they always had big fluffy biscuits and on occasion, cinnamon rolls.

Finally, grabbing the cookies Nead had helped her bake the night before, along with her books and lunch bag, Lillian rushed Littie, Nead and Jennie out the door, pushed Gladys back inside because she wasn't old enough to go to school yet, and they all practically ran over Lula on the front steps, the boys making giant leaps over the heads of the little ones to avoid a real collision.

"Whoa!" cried Lula. "Hold your horses. This is a big day for Randolph too, you know, being his first day working in the mines and all." So all the children chimed in congratulations and best wishes and be carefuls, but it was really Lula who wanted that last few minutes with her son. She shooed the others on their way with pats on their behinds, pats on the head, and kisses then hugged Randolph with all her might.

"Mama, I'm just going to work. I'll be back for supper!"

"It's a big step you're taking, Son," she said quietly, knowing that he could choose another direction and neither she nor William could stop him. So many of the young men were leaving their families and heading up north to find work, but Randolph wanted to be close home and close to his father at work.

He kissed her goodbye and ran to catch the others for their lengthy walk out of the holler. At the top of the hill they separated, calling their goodbyes and again wishing each other a good day. Randolph held back and whispered wickedly to Lillian, "I'll get those ribbons tomorrow. You just watch!" She was still grinning when she slid into her seat at school - just in the nick of time.

Morning recess was generally so short that the students found they couldn't really get involved in a good rousing game of softball or even marbles, so they just stood around in groups talking about work, hunting, illnesses, or maybe new babies in the community, all according to whether you were a boy or a girl. Lillian stood under the giant oak trees that bordered the playground with a group of the other girls who were stamping their feet and breathing on their hands to keep warm. She moved closer to her friend, Corrie Whitaker, a ninth grader, and rather casually asked the age-old question that everyone ended up asking all the older girls sooner or later. "Do you think you'll come back next year?"

Corrie blushed and ducked her head slightly. "Oh Lil, I'll be lucky to finish out this year!" Her violet eyes sparkled as she continued in a whisper that only Lillian could hear, "Billy and me got married over Thanksgiving break so I'm Mrs. William Franklin Harris now, and, well," she opened her coat so that Lillian could see her slightly swollen belly, "now there's the baby!" Lillian gasped, but Corrie shushed her. "Only our families know."

Lillian said, "I'm happy for you, Corrie. You know, about the baby and all." She gave the girl a quick hug.

Corrie wrapped her coat tighter around her middle and prattled on. "I know it won't be easy, but I do plan to keep reading and studying at home."

Lillian agreed that continuing her studies was a great idea. But her thoughts had already turned inward as she studied the tops of the magnificent oaks for a few seconds, letting her mind wander to all the days she had played school with the younger kids at home, teaching them not only the three R's but the love of God and man interwoven between the lines.

Suddenly she announced to anyone who would listen, "I'm coming back." Then she stated it again, a little more enthusiastically, "I'm coming back! I've always wanted to be a teacher and there's so much I don't know. I can't quit now!" The excitement in her voice carried through the group and they all turned to gape at her.

"Lillie, calm down," Corrie teased. "I'm happy for you, too, but you've got plenty of time to decide things like that!"

They looked up and saw their teacher, Mrs. Leonard, crossing the playground, heading straight for them.

"What now?" Helen James, the oldest girl in the group, asked between clenched teeth. "She's been on our case all year."

When Mrs. Leonard was within hearing distance she called to Lillian. The other girls sighed with relief and Corrie pushed Lillian forward, with a whispered, "Go!"

Mrs. Leonard didn't say another word until they had reached the principal's office. Lillian was confused, especially seeing Nead, Littie and Jennie standing by the principal's imposing mahogany desk. "Why are my sisters here? What's going on?"

"Your mother sent word that you should come home now," the teacher said, and pointing to the children, she finished quietly, "and bring them with you."

"But she knew I was getting out early today - something's wrong, isn't it?" Lillian swallowed down the fear that threatened to choke her. In all the years she had been in school Lula had never sent for her so it had to be something bad, but for the children's sake she had to control the panic that was eating at her. With a pretense that took all her strength, she gathered the girls around her and whispered that things would be fine.

The principal leaned forward over the desk, and, nodding toward the younger ones, said, "Take them home, sweetheart. You'll know soon enough."

When they had bundled up as warmly as possible, they left the school building, stepping out onto the crusty snow and ice. Jennie started to cry but the others quickly teased her out of it, afraid her face truly would freeze. Nead, being thirteen that year, thought she understood the situation. "Lil, I'll see to the girls. You walk on ahead and see what's happened." Her voice was barely above a whisper but Lillian heard and was grateful. She hugged all three of them, then took off in a run, slipping and sliding but managing to stay on her feet.

A mighty wind followed her in the back door. Neither of her parents were anywhere on the lower floor, but she could see her Aunt Lena through the kitchen window, fighting the wind while trying to hang wet clothes on the frozen line. Lillian watched as Lena suddenly dropped the last shirt back into the basket and started walking as fast as possible toward the younger children. Lillian sighed with relief, happy that someone else was in charge of them. She could hear their excited chatter as they reached the end of the driveway. She knew their aunt was telling them something to distract them from whatever news they were going to hear. Starting their lessons was the best thing for them right now and Nead would definitely take charge of that and give them a snack, leaving Lena to care for the babies, Joe and Gladys.

Going straight upstairs, she found that Lula had taken to her bed, but William was nowhere to be found. She tiptoed into the darkened room, frightened by her mother's heartbreaking moans.

"Mama? What is it?" Lillian sat on the edge of the bed and smoothed the beautiful, soft brown hair back from her mother's tear-stained face. Lula's swollen eyes were closed tightly as if to shut out the awful thing that had taken place. The moans escaped from lips that were pale and white. "Shh," Lillian crooned. "Don't cry, Mama. It can't be that bad." Lillian had spent the long sprint through the snow and ice trying to put a name to whatever tragedy had occurred and then convinced herself that it was something like a sick headache or maybe a fight with Daddy. Such are the thoughts of a fourteen-year-old child.

Finally, Lula sat up and threw back the covers, struggling to get to her feet. Screaming to no one and about nothing, she finally managed to stand and take a few steps toward the door.

Lillian stepped in front of her and wrapped her arms around the trembling body. "Mama, what's happened? Where are you going?"

"My baby! I need to get to my baby," Lula cried pitifully. "They won't let me see my little boy!" She rested her head on Lillian's shoulder, and although Lillian could not imagine what her mother's words meant, she cried, too. *What could break my mother's heart like this?*

After a few more moments, Lula's knees refused to hold her up any longer so Lillian caught her and eased her back onto the bed and sat beside her, gently holding her work-worn hand. "Mama, tell me."

"There was an accident," Lula finally managed to say. "Our Randolph is dead."

Randolph? My precious brother? His very first day in the mines? Lillian's head was spinning but she knew she couldn't ask any more of her mother. She eased the heartbroken woman back into bed, carefully tucking the quilt beneath her on both sides so she couldn't easily get up again, and then went back downstairs quietly, intending to find William. Halfway down, she saw that Nead had helped the girls peel off their coats and hats, and given them a warm snack. They were all sitting at the kitchen table, diligently working on their lessons, just as Lillian had thought. She smiled in spite of herself as she heard Nead telling the others, "Now, I'm the oldest so I'm in charge." For some reason there was no argument.

When Lillian reached the bottom step, she collided with her Aunt Lena, tip-toeing out of the babies' bedroom.

"Oh, child. What can I say?" Lena's tears spilled down the back of Lillian's dress as they hugged each other. Lena held Lillian tightly, seemingly never to let go. Lillian had always been close to Lena, her mother's sister, so she drew comfort from her now. She was just as loving, caring and fair as Lula and Lillian loved her dearly. She and her husband, Charles, lived on a farm a few miles away and Lillian had always enjoyed spending time there.

"You can stay and help with the babies?" Lillian asked, and Lena nodded. Jennie would have kicked some shins if she had heard herself being called a baby but it was easier for Lillian to lump them into one category rather than name them.

Her thoughts ran rampant as Aunt Lena spoke of the accident. "In the mine?" she asked through her tears. "On the way home? Oh, God, was he leaving early because of me and made a mistake?" She felt her heart tear in two at the very thought. Randolph had always celebrated with her for every little accomplishment in her life. Even an early dismissal for Valentine's Day would have brought him running. "Was it because he was coming for me?" Lillian asked.

Lena assured her it had nothing to do with her. "Although I know he wanted to be here." Lena swallowed hard and continued with the little bit of information she had. "It was falling slate that caught him in such a way there was nothing any of them could do." She finished in a whisper, "They said he didn't suffer at all."

Big brother no more. Her hero gone. Never would she hear his voice again or see his smiling face. How could she bear it? After the longest time, Lillian looked up and asked, "Where's Daddy?" She looked around the room as if seeing it for the first time. "And Dewey?"

"Dewey's helping at the mine, but nobody's seen your daddy since the sheriff left."

Lillian nodded, knowing that was typical of her father. "I'll find him later."

Without a backward glance, Lillian grabbed her coat and hat and was out the door within seconds, headed for the spring, tears blinding her every step of the way. She practically slid down the hill, but the spring was calling her even more than usual.

The only place on the farm I never shared with Randolph, she thought as she reached her favorite rock, now shiny with a thin film of ice on the moss. "He always had other chores and places to go," she told herself, running all her memories through her mind like the movie reel she'd seen in Harriman a year or two ago. She remembered the way he had carried her across the creek when they went fishing, the rough feel of his overalls against her cheek, the sight of him working alongside Daddy to get the potatoes planted, hoed, dug, and hauled to the school to sell. She smiled now at the memory of him kissing Mama every time he left the house, even if he was just going for a wagonload of firewood and would be right back. Sometimes he would "haul" her and some of the younger children up to the high wagon seat and let them ride along. Oh, Randy, how can I go on without you?

She slowly, carefully climbed the hill, refusing to pause at the stopping place for a break. Desperate to see how her father was holding up and needing to be comforted in his strong arms, she searched the barn and the shed, calling his name as she went. Finally, she remembered the cellar; cold, damp and dark. William sat with his knees drawn up and his head down. Lillian could feel his shoulders trembling as he shed tears for his son. Now, once again, the child became the comforter for the parent. "Don't cry Daddy," she pleaded, "Mama needs you to be strong."

After a while, he slowly raised his head and wiped the tears on his coat sleeve. "I know, child, but it hurts so bad." They nodded their heads in agreement and crawled out into the brightness of the day, the sun and wind in a fierce battle for control. Never again did father and daughter feel such closeness. Never again would they expose their inner feelings to each other in such a way. Now Lillian led the way into the warmth of the house, finally able to greet everyone with a smile.

They were especially comforted by all the mourners who came to pay their respects. Archibald and Martha Adcock had been pillars of the community and the loss of a grandson deserved public condolences. Miners from surrounding areas had heard the news and came, if only to stand quietly, grieving at the loss of one of their own.

The service was delayed as long as possible, waiting for Evan and his new bride, Grace, to arrive, but they had to move forward, so Dewey offered his arm to his mother and walked her to the front of the church and sat her next to his wife, Hazel. William waited until the last moment then joined Lula on the front pew. Hazel moved over a little, making room for Papaw Fry. He sat quietly, tears streaming down his wrinkled face, holding tightly to Lula's hand. Lillian and her sisters, having never attended a funeral before, sat in the next pew, in total awe of all the people and the preacher's loud rantings. Soon it was over and they had to face life without Randolph.

Randolph Hobart Adcock, nineteen years of age, was laid to rest in the Adcock family cemetery ... brother, son, and hero - gone but not forgotten.

The days, the weeks, the months were a struggle for the entire family, but more so for Lillian because, along with the emptiness in her heart, she was faced with the decision of whether to return to school, now or ever. Lula and William were broken souls and it seemed they couldn't carry on. Who would care for them? The decision was made for her when Lula announced quietly that she was pregnant again. Life must go on and if it meant staying home to care for her family and welcome a precious new little one into the world, then so be it. Lillian, at age fifteen, and of her own free will, ended her formal education

The children balked at having to face school without their big sister, but she smiled, patted them on their heads absent-mindedly and sent them away, alienating herself more every day. By her own choice, her days were spent following William and Lula around the house and farm, trying to make herself useful, hoping there might be some way she could take Randolph's place. But she was reminded constantly that it wasn't possible. "Never again," bellowed the thunder that hid behind the April showers. "He's gone," whispered the early May flowers. Even her beloved spring tortured her with, "Too late, too late!" as its clear water rippled over the rocks and disappeared around the curve of the mountain. Her heart ached. Her face burned with the tears that so easily flowed. Her knees hurt from the days she fell on them begging God to give her back her brother or at least ease the pain of losing him—asking God to promise that she would see him again when Jesus comes in clouds of glory to claim His own.

We don't like to acknowledge it, but time does ease the pain of loss. Our system simply has no choice except to say, "Okay, it's live or die." And we choose to live. Such was the decision for Lillian. She awakened early one morning thinking to walk the fields aimlessly, nurturing her suffering and sorrow, but some little spark deep inside her soul came alive and then there was fire, a vitality, a little zest for life, whatever it offered. A smile, a giggle, a laugh. Then bubbling curiosity about the surprises of this day.

"Jennie! Last call before I get the cold water." Lillian had encouraged her sisters to get to bed early at night so they wouldn't have such a hard time getting up for school but so far nothing was working. Now she stood in the room that the four of them shared and began her daily ritual. "Nead, you should already have your chores done by now. Come on, girl! Littie, up and at 'em! Mama's counting on you to help with the washing today!" Only Gladys was spared.

Then she heard giggling under the covers. *What now?*

All four girls popped up at once, clamoring for a hug from their sister. As soon as they were wrapped in her arms, they cried in unison, "It's Saturday!" laughing at the crimson stain of embarrassment creeping across Lillian's face.

"It is?" Her days had been tedious and jumbled together for so long, she realized she really didn't know which day was which. Gathering her wits about her, she tightened her arms around the girls and apologized for waking them on a Saturday when chores were excused for a couple of hours. "Go back to sleep if you want."

But they had other ideas. "We don't want to sleep," Nead informed her. "We want to go to Aunt Lena and Uncle Charles' house and we want you to go with us!"

Lillian had hardly seen her favorite aunt and uncle, and certainly hadn't been to visit them in several months even though they just lived around the corner. It had just not been in her to face anyone, but now it sounded like a good idea. "What about breakfast?" she asked.

"Aunt Lena's fixing it for us!" The girls were up and ready now, eager for the day's adventures. "We get to ride the new pony, and Uncle Charles is taking us to the store for candy and …."

"So you had this all planned out, huh? Very funny." Lillian could only shake her head. *I gotta get a life.* But she did enjoy the day, especially when they all piled into the old rattle-trap of a truck that Uncle Charles kept just for hauling groceries and went to the store. Lillian didn't buy any candy but the others insisted on sharing with her, then they all saved some for Mama and Daddy. Lillian saved two pieces that were soft enough for Joe and Gladys. Everyone went home with groceries in their laps because there was no room anywhere else. They declared the candy delicious.

Within a year of Randolph's tragic death, their lives had returned to what the family deemed normal; official mourning was over even if their hearts still ached for Randolph's laughter or his footstep. The family began to venture out into the community again.

Lillian had longed to see her friend Corrie Whitaker, now Harris, but simply hadn't had the strength to make the effort. Now, she climbed the rickety front steps at the Whitaker place, hoping to learn where Corrie lived. The door swung open before she had even knocked and

Adele Whitaker, Corrie's mother, announced angrily that whatever she was selling they didn't need any.

"No, no!" Lillian stammered. "I'm her … we're … I'm Lillian Adcock. I went to school with Corrie and just wanted to visit for a minute. Can you tell me where she lives now?"

The woman made a scoffing sound. "Yeah, I can tell you where she lives. Little Miss Hoity-Toity has been knocked off her high horse!" She seemed to regret the words as soon as they were out of her mouth, so she moved aside and gestured for Lillian to come in. "She's in there in the back room."

Lillian eased the ragged screen door open and slipped inside, directly into the living room. "I'm sorry I didn't bring anything. I was just out walking and decided to …."

Adele interrupted her. "No different than anybody else around here. They's all alike – swarming around when you don't need 'em and like ghosts when you do." She rambled on, disappearing through the back door, leaving Lillian to find her way in the filth that was called home.

Lillian stood still, waiting for her eyes to adjust to the semi-darkness, then moved quietly toward an open door to her right. Peeking inside, she gasped and turned back so quickly she tripped over a small toy that made a squeaking sound. There was a man in that bed, mumbling in his sleep! Her heart pounding and embarrassment spreading all over her body, she reached for the front door.

"Lillian?" Suddenly Corrie appeared from a room that Lillian hadn't been able to see. "What are you doing here?"

Lillian usually found herself taking blame for anything and everything that went wrong, but she suddenly realized that wanting to visit your friend couldn't be that bad so she put a little spunk in her voice. "I was just asking your mother where you lived now – I hadn't heard anything since ...."

"Yeah, well," the girl said, studying the worn floor as if words were written there for her to pass on. "You may as well know – Billy left me so I had to move back here." She spread her arms to indicate what was included in "here" – dirty clothes were piled in every corner of the room, dishes left from several days before were scattered about. The February sun pushed faint rays of light through the greasy, unwashed windows, revealing cobwebs and dust claiming every free space and seeking more.

"I'm sorry," Lillian began, but Corrie stopped her with a hand in the air.

"Don't you dare feel sorry for me! I made my bed and I have to lay in it," she said with a choked laugh. "At least that's what Mama's been saying every day since I came back. I guess I believe it by now."

Lillian managed to reach her friend and wrap her in a hug. "Corrie, there's a difference in compassion and pity. I just meant that I was sorry your plans got changed." Her voice faltered and the tears flowed freely. "My plans were changed, too."

"I know," Corrie said quietly. "I'm sorry."

They giggled in spite of their heartache. "You see," Lillian pointed out – "not pity, just caring."

"Do you wanna see the light of my life?"

"Not if it's in this room," Lillian whispered, gesturing toward the bedroom she had peeked into.

Corrie reached over and closed the bedroom door. "No," she said, stifling a laugh, "that's my daddy. He works at the saw mill over on Fairview Road. It's his day off." She wrinkled her nose in disgust at the man who slept unkempt in the room Lillian had seen.

They made their way to a room that wasn't much bigger than a closet and Corrie gently pushed the door open. There in the middle of a small mattress on the floor lay an absolute angel, perfectly formed, blond curls framing his beautiful little face, six-month-old William Franklin Harris III, sleeping peacefully.

Lillian was awed. She put her hand over her mouth as if to keep the words of praise trapped inside.

"Oh, Corrie. He's …." Lillian whispered. "I've never seen such a pretty baby!" It was true. She considered all babies to be pretty but any she had ever been around, including her own brothers, sisters and cousins, had dark hair and eyes. What a refreshing difference, she thought. I had forgotten about Billy's fair coloring.

Still whispering, Lillian asked, "Blue eyes?"

Corrie laughed and nodded vigorously, as if that would describe just how blue they were. But then she sobered. "When Billy left, I thought I would die but the worst part was knowing that Little Billy would grow up without a daddy."

Before Lillian could help herself, she blurted out, "How could a daddy walk out on such a precious little guy?"

"Well, I have to take some of the blame, too," Corrie said in typical woman fashion. "We lived in a nasty little place to be close to his work and I guess I nagged a lot. Anyway, he started drinking and it just all fell apart." She bent to straighten the threadbare blanket around the baby's feet and smiled. "I think if Little Billy wasn't such a good baby, Mama would kick us out of here. She don't like her plans being changed either."

The entire outing had been disturbing to Lillian. When she reached the farm, in spite of a biting winter wind and pitifully weak sunshine, she turned left at the top of the hill and hurried down to the spring, finding that her rock had become the victim of a fallen spruce limb. When she finally was able to sit and rest, she realized she was really concerned about Corrie. Of course the girl, no, she's a woman now,

Lillian reminded herself, had reason to be depressed but it must have gone further than that for the Whitaker's house to be in such a state, inside and out. What was wrong with those people? And she knew for sure and certain that Billy had not started drinking after they got married but why say anything?

When she had readied herself to leave the Whitakers, she had asked Corrie if there was anything she could do to help, had even volunteered her own mother's help, but the answer was a cold shoulder.

"Okay, Lillian," Randolph spoke from his special place in the depths of her heart, "the best thing you can do is help the ones who really need it and will accept it." *Thanks, Brother. That's exactly what I will do!*

1918

This summer had come and gone quickly. The blooming garden that they had all worked in at one time or another became a promise of food for the coming winter. Okra was breaded and fried and quickly became a favorite dish for now and pickled and canned for later. Green beans were gathered and threaded on strings to hang from the attic to make leather britches. Tomatoes were canned by the dozens and sat next to the poke salad in the cellar. Potatoes would soon be brought to the cellar and covered in hay and used sparingly over the next few months, for they had few staples to get them through the winter. They looked forward to storing pumpkins and turnips but since these were also used to feed the farm animals, they used those sparingly, too.

Lillian had just celebrated her sixteenth birthday with the old saying 'sweet sixteen and never been kissed' running through her head. There had been cake and simple handmade gifts from her brothers and a truly lovely turquoise pendant from her deceased grandparents, Martha and Archibald Adcock, which William had hidden away for her for this very day. Aunt Lena had made her a dress that matched her coloring perfectly, in earthy colors of varying shades of brown, along with a pinafore done in light gold, and a darker gold ribbon running across the hem. Her sisters had pooled their pitiful savings and bought her a long, flowing scarf done in soft yellows and oranges, with just a touch of brilliant red.

Lula had taken her daughter aside and presented her with a beautiful blue blanket and a pillow for her bed. The pillowcase was embroidered with bluebirds and cherry blossoms, two of Lillian's favorite things. "Oh, Mama, how did you ...?" Lula stopped her with a kiss on her brow and wished her the happiest birthday ever.

But it wasn't and they all knew it. When she arose this day, Lillian glanced out the bedroom window in time to see the doctor leaving the farm after a house call to see her precious little sister Littie, now twelve years old, who had been sick for several days. They had tried every home remedy they and others knew about and she was just getting worse. Lillian dressed quickly, and, taking the stairs two at a time, rushed into the kitchen and found her mother sitting at the table. Lula, looking beaten, held her head in her hands. "What did the doctor say, Mama?" Lillian asked quietly.

"It ain't good, daughter. He says it's typhoid and he'll be surprised if we don't all come down with it."

Instinctively, Lillian hurried to find Nead, Jennie and Gladys, knowing they too would be frightened. Maybe her love would be enough to protect them. She found all three of them huddled together on the floor outside Littie's room.

"Come on, girls, let's find something to keep our minds and hands busy, okay?" she said, pulling Gladys to her feet. Nead and Jennie followed obediently. Lillian led them through the kitchen and toward the back door.

"Take your brother with you, too, Lil," Lula called, so they added four-year-old Joe to their gang and continued out to the porch. Now what? They finally decided on a ride in the row boat on the pond. But it was a long walk.

Nead, evidently deciding that the atmosphere was just a little too somber, began to sing in her clear, sweet voice, 'Old Mac Donald'. The others laughed but not in a very nice way. "Well, you pick one, smarty," she said, glaring at Lillian.

"I'm sorry, Nead," Lillian said. "I don't know why it struck me as funny. But I sure got a lesson in setting a good example, didn't I? Little pitchers have big ears!" They giggled at that as they tried to figure out a good song that Gladys and Joe could sing, too. Finally Joe piped up. "But I like Old Mac Donald," he shrieked and stomped his little foot on the dry, hard ground. Nead just smiled and began again.

The kitchen was quiet after the children left. With her heart breaking, Lula knew she still had to stay on her feet to cook for the family, keep the house clean, the clothes scrubbed and ironed, and now care for her ailing daughter. Even though all the older children pitched in, especially helping care for their sweet new baby, Vernal, it was still more than Lula could bear.

"I need help, Lord," she whispered reverently. Her knees ached from arthritis but she knelt beside her chair and begged for her daughter's life and more help around the house. "If it be your will, Lord."

At the dinner table the next evening, William kept glancing at his wife as if she had gravy on her chin. "What?" she finally asked.

"You just look different. Did you catch up on your sleep?"

Although Lula knew what made her look different, she chose not to share. During the night she had had a most wonderful dream – God had actually told her that everything was going to be alright. "Trust me," He had said. Now in the light of day she felt a little foolish to put so much faith in a dream but she couldn't just ignore the feeling of assurance she felt. God was in charge of everything else – why not this? So she put her daughter in His hands and went about the business of caring for her family. She smiled at her husband and said, "Have some more coffee, dear."

They laid Littie V. Adcock to rest in the family cemetery a couple of days after Christmas, a twelve-year-old forever destined to be a child, never blossoming into the woman she might have been. *Sleep well, beloved daughter and sister. Sleep well. We will meet again.*

Over the next few wintry months, Lillian kept her pain and disappointment to herself for she too had prayed that God would spare Littie's life, a child, so innocent, such a vital part of their family. "Please, Lord, make her well and healthy again and I will give You all the praise." Now, with nothing but chores to distract her from heartbreaking thoughts, no plans for a better life, no real hope for the future, healing from another death seemed impossible. Her beloved spring had become an altar of sorts, a place where she could worship, praising God, even during trying circumstances. Her many trips there that winter taught her to lay it all in God's hands. Eventually she allowed God to enter her heart and began to feel His love bubbling up from the earth into her very being. *My precious Littie, I will never forget you.* Slowly Lillian began to heal. Again.

1920

"What else did you put in it?" Jennie sidled up to the cabinet to sneak a peek into Lillian's picnic basket. Lula was under the weather so the girls had finished her chores along with their own and Lillian was planning an outing to the church with Lena and Charles. She brushed her long brown hair back from her face and even in her excitement tried to be patient with her sister.

"Be careful, Jennie. You break one of those glass doors and, well, you know what Daddy will do." The white wood cabinet with the glass doors in the upper section had been in William's family as long as he could remember and since his parents' death, it belonged to him and his family. He and Lula expected the children to respect and care for all the household furnishings but especially this piece. When he had first brought it home, they had scoffed a little, thinking they had seen all there was to see when it was at Mamaw and Papaw's house.

William, just a little bit miffed, waited two whole years before he took time to turn the cabinet around and show them the back panel where his mother had kept a chart of the family's heights – there was William, growing by leaps and bounds with his brothers Pleasant and James lagging a little behind, and his sisters Luiza and Mary Ann, well, he had always called them "short stuff." His children were impressed.

"I'm being just as careful as you are, Lillian Adcock!" Jennie defended herself. "Now, what's in there?"

"There's three ham and egg biscuits, two apples, two cookies, some grapes off your vine and some of that sarsaparilla Daddy bought last week." Lillian described everything in the basket as if she hadn't been interrupted.

Jennie's eyes widened. "You better be glad Mama's not in here, young lady! And whad'ya mean taking grapes off my vine?"

But Lillian was already out the door, headed for the end of the driveway to wait for Uncle Charles' buggy, pulled by their mighty stallion, Kingpin. She carefully placed the basket at her feet and sat quietly on the rather prickly grass, contemplating the rest of her day at the church. It was the annual "Box Supper Social" and it was the first time she had been allowed to go without her parents. Oh, there would be plenty of adult supervision, what with her many aunts and uncles there, but she was hoping that a certain young man would buy her picnic and they could spend some quiet time alone. So far, being eighteen had held none of the fun she had heard about.

She saw the dust boiling up long before Kingpin came into view and stepped back away from the road, trying to protect her freshly washed clothes and polished shoes. It was no use but then it occurred to her that everyone else would be just as dusty in this dry weather. All the old-timers at the store said it was the worst drought they had ever lived through so nobody could be outside and stay clean. The horse finally slowed and Uncle Charles brought the buggy to a stop directly in front of Lillian. Easing down heavily, he came around to help with her precious load. In a flash, she had kissed his whiskered cheek, climbed aboard and they were off. She turned just in time to see Jennie waving from the front window but not in time to wave back. I can't be worrying about that now! She and Lena chatted all the way to the church but as soon as Kingpin came to a halt in front of the side door, Lillian, holding tightly to her basket, helped herself down before Uncle Charles had a chance and, with a quick wave to Lena, disappeared into the building.

She had met Scott Wiggins, a tall, heavyweight sort of guy, a month before when they had both showed up at a school function, Scott following around after his nephew, Martin, and she with Jennie. One of the teachers had introduced them but for the life of her, Lillian couldn't tell you which one because she was smitten, and even now was slightly breathless at the thought of seeing him again. She had immediately noticed his coal-black hair, just the slightest bit too long so that it curled over the collar of his blue gabardine shirt. She loved the way he dipped his head to hear what Martin had to say. Oh, to be that close to ….

Suddenly they were calling for the ladies to place their baskets on the table up front and everyone to be seated. Lillian's already-short fingernails were now being chewed even shorter and to her dismay she found she was perspiring! Not now, please! Well, it was just her upper lip and she could remedy that with her hankie. What hankie? She must have lost it! Quickly finding a seat beside Corrie Whitaker or whatever her name was now, she sat nervously twisting the belt on her dress until it resembled a frayed rope. She heard heavy footsteps coming closer, then a chair seemed to move on its own and stop beside her. Looking up, and up, she drew in a sharp breath, mostly because Corrie had jabbed her in the ribs from the other side but mainly because the man in the chair was none other than Scott!

1921

"I tell you, Lena, it has to be a boy. She goes around all dreamy-eyed, forgetting her chores, even forgetting to eat! I don't know what to do."

Lena leaned over and brushed the green bean strings from her apron into the lard can that William would empty into the garden later. The sisters had been working all morning to get a canning ready, and now it was time for Lena to head home and prepare dinner for her family. "Lula, I don't think there's anything you can do," she said. "It's just something you have to weather through." She gathered up her hat, and her bucket of beans that Lula had shared and headed for the door, then turned back. "I need one more sip of water if you don't mind."

"Welcome to it," Lula said. "Do you want to take a piece or two of this cake with you?"

"Best not. I've already let this dress out twice!" They laughed together as Lena returned the dipper to the hanger on the wall and carefully covered the bucket of water with a clean dish towel. Still seemingly reluctant to leave, she leaned against the door a few moments then finally spoke up. "I've been thinking, Lu. This might be a good time for Lillian to come and stay with me for a few weeks. There's plenty there to keep her busy, you know, get her mind off whoever this boy is. I'll bet she would be a different person by the time she got back."

Lula made a snorting sound. "I didn't say I wanted a different person! I just don't think she's growed up enough to be thinking about marriage and family!"

"Who said anything about marriage? Besides just who was it that got married before they was twenty?"

"Both of us!" Laughter rang out again but Lula was not convinced Lillian going away was the answer. "I'll talk to William," she said, discreetly spitting into her snuff jar, and that ended the conversation.

But Lillian did go a-visiting. Aunt Lena and her husband, Charles, lived on a farm a few miles away. At first, Lillian was homesick and spent some time moping, walking the fields, and hiding in the barn loft. Her cousin, Oscar, was spending time with the Clarks, too, but Lillian mostly ignored him. If she had been looking for a friend, she probably would have chosen her cousin Crowder, Lena and Charles' son, but they all seemed to be content in their own little worlds.

Then slowly Lillian began to notice things around her, the pond sparkling in the moonlight, flowers that Aunt Lena had planted along the path to the spring, the sound of the guinea hens as they pecked around in the dewy grass, and the light of Aunt Lena and Uncle Charles' life, their baby girl, Helen, who was just starting to walk and talk.

One morning, Lena found Lillian gathering eggs. Lillian grinned sheepishly. "I thought I'd better start pulling my weight," she said, slipping two warm, brown eggs into her pocket.

"Plenty of time for that, but you'll need a basket for those before you're finished." Lena turned back to the barn and came out carrying two baskets. "These were my mother's," she said quietly. "I'll help you – I know where all the nests are." They finished in the barn, crossed over the dusty driveway to the henhouse, and continued around the edges of the garden, finding a nest every few feet.

"Hens are silly," Lillian said, mostly to herself. "At home they will lay anywhere besides where you want them to." At the mention of home, her eyes filled with scalding tears. She blinked them away but not quickly enough.

"There's more to it than just missing your family, isn't there?" Lena had held her tongue long enough – it was plain the girl was hurting. "You're in love?"

"Oh, Aunt Lena, I think Mama and Daddy made me come here just to get me away from him. Not that I don't like being with you and Uncle Charles and the baby and the farm is beautiful and …."

Lena set her basket of eggs down and took Lillian in her arms. "My sweet child, you don't have to explain. Your folks didn't make you come – I invited you, but you're right, it was to try to help you search your heart and decide what you really want in life, and to know how to appreciate the opportunities you have. Just a little room to grow, you know?"

Lillian wiped her face with her checkered apron. "You mean grow up? But why couldn't I do that at home?"

"Were you? Seemed to all of us you were just pining away, no direction, no answers."

"Well, I have been doing a lot of thinking since I've been here. In my mind I do have some direction, some of the answers." She smiled at her aunt and they started back toward the house, arm in arm. "By the way, I'd like to look after Helen for you this afternoon if you have something else you need to do."

"I can think of a few things," Lena said with a laugh. "There's something I need to tell you, though. Your mother is pregnant. Yes, again," she added at the incredulous expression on Lillian's face. "And the doctor doesn't think it's going well."

Lillian immediately regretted her first thoughts of criticism. Who could ever have too many babies? And who was she to judge? "I think I should get on home pretty soon, Aunt Lena," she said thoughtfully. "I'll do everything I can to help Mama."

By the time Lillian had reached home and settled in again, she had made up her mind. Cornering Lula as they finished up their chores one day about a week later, she announced in a squeaky voice, "I'm going to marry him, Mama."

Lula took a few more swipes with the mop on the rough floor before answering. "Well," she said finally, "the heart wants what the heart wants, daughter. When will the wedding be?"

"Gracious, Mama! He hasn't even asked me yet!" But Lillian's eyes sparkled. She knew that somehow, some way she would manage to get a proposal out of Thomas Scott Wiggins before long!

But the ugly shadow of death hangs ever near, and, in spite of everyone's efforts, they laid their precious newborn son, nephew and brother, Wayne London Adcock to rest in the Adcock family cemetery. May he rest in peace until Jesus comes.

Then again, there seems to be a time in all our lives when things quiet down and good things do happen – cherished occasions that make the load easier, smiles more frequent. Ordinary daily life goes on, but precious needs and wants of the heart snuggle into the nooks and crannies of time.

Nead flopped down on the bed next to her sister, pushing aside a worn copy of Gray's Anatomy that Lillian had been reading late into the night. They had been out back all morning, picking blackberries and were trying to cool off. "We could go to the spring," Nead offered.

"No, I'd never make it back up the hill," Lillian whined. "At least we get cobbler for supper, though."

"It won't be as good unless we convince Jennie and Gladys to go to the spring to get the cream. They could take Joe and throw him in." Even though she was smiling, Nead's words sounded cruel to Lillian.

"Hey! Don't talk like that, Vaneda. Sometimes you can make things happen - like an inside wish or something."

"You know very well I was teasing. I love little Joe – much more than I love you, smarty-pants," Nead said, grabbing a pillow and pretending to smother her sister. By the time they had finished their scuffle, the beautiful chintz bedspread, with its lavender roses in the middle, two pillows and one sheet were in a heap on the floor with the girls on top.

Lillian gasped. "We can't let Mama see this! Get up and help me!" She tried pulling Nead up by an arm but when she looked down she saw that the girl was crying. "Oh, sweetheart. Did I hurt you? I'm so sorry."

But Nead continued to bawl. Lillian was ready to go find help when Nead managed to speak. "I'm going to miss you, Lilly."

"What?" Lillian pushed until Nead was off the bed covers and began putting the bed back in order. "That's why you're crying?" She started to laugh it off then decided that they really needed to talk and sat back down on the floor.

"Honey, it's not like I'm going to the moon or something. We'll still be sisters."

"It won't be the same and you know it. I mean, I like Scott and all, but now if I want to see you I gotta come to your house like a, like a guest." She buried her face on her sister's shoulder and wailed.

"Nead, you have to look on the bright side. Guess who's gonna be the oldest when I'm gone? Huh?" She poked her sister in the ribs. "You get to be the boss and I know you've been practicing 'cause yesterday Jennie asked me if you had swallowed a porcupine!"

Nead grinned, remembering when she'd tried to make Jennie do her ironing for her. "Well, maybe there are some good things about it," she agreed.

"Change is good."

"So, what do you think married life will be like? Seems like you're just gonna be doing the same old things you do here – carry water, do the dishes, cook – what's so different about marriage?"

Lillian blushed head to toe, trying to cover her face with the now-rumpled sheet. "Let's get this bed made then I will take Joe to the spring to get the cream."

"Thought you were too tired."

"Well, I suddenly got a burst of energy."

The cobbler, made by the best cook in the world, was delicious. Thanks, Mama.

Gone now were the days of carefree childhood, climbing trees, playing hide-and-seek in the barn, flopping on her tummy to dabble her fingers in the cold spring water and giggling at frogs. Gone were the plans for higher education, if they had been considered at all. Lillian didn't resent the losses but relished her role as a wife to her beloved Scott, spending long hours at the stove to cook his favorite meals, carrying load after load of icy water from the spring to make sure his clothes were clean, and then sleeping beside his warm body at night.

People, including her own family, had cautioned her about marrying someone who had been disabled by a war injury like Scott had. The most frequent warning had been, "You'll have to be the breadwinner, Lillian. He's disabled - he'll never be able to support you, much less a family."

Lillian had paid no heed to the naysayers, so, in September they had been married in a quiet ceremony with only select family present. For some it was a hardship to travel so they sent their best wishes and an occasional house-warming gift.

William and Lula had made arrangements for Scott and Lillian to own the little house and land across the road from the family cemetery. It was a generous gesture, but, even though the fruit and nut trees were mature and producing grandly, it still involved back-breaking work. In comparison to farms around them, theirs would have been considered tiny but it was theirs and they worked hard to build it up.

The house itself was not much to look at, but it served its purpose. Furnishings were handed down from parents and grandparents, friends, and neighbors. "Look what I found in my attic!" "Did you see those curtains Aunt Paula sewed for the fair? Maybe you should ask her to …."

Lillian knew nothing of a hope chest or dowry but she had spent a lot of time sewing, embroidering, and even crocheting during her times of mourning, thinking she would pass a few things on to her sisters. Lula thought to round out the medley with some trappings of her own so she, and her sisters had been busy, needle and thread gliding in and out, in and out, day and night.

This was harvest week so Lillian had been helping William gather the pumpkins and winter squash from his garden. Nead and Jennie were supposed to be placing them in the cellar but they were giggling and goofing off so much Lillian was afraid William would get rough with them. "Girls!" Her firm voice startled them so at least she had their attention. Gesturing toward their father, she said, "I'm afraid you're going to get your hides tanned if you don't behave."

Jennie was quick on the draw. "You're not the boss of me," she spat at her sister.

"Ouch," Lillian said, pretending she had been struck. "Of course, I'm not. I was just trying to save you from a whipping. Go ahead and splash pumpkins all over the place and see if I care!" Kids! Lillian turned and practically ran for the house, hoping to find a cool drink. Lula found her stretched out on the living room floor with her feet propped on the wall. She handed her daughter a glass of buttermilk that had been chilling in the spring.

"Get your dirty feet off my wall, child," she said in mock fierceness, because it was obvious that Lillian had removed her shoes.

"Mama, do you think I'll be a good wife and mother?"

Lula set her drink on the side table and crossed her arms over her ample bosom. "Little late for asking that, aint it? Maybe you should have come to me last year when you was moping around like a sick puppy."

Lillian's heart sank – what if Mama was right and she had forged ahead on her own, stubborn as a mule? She didn't ask anyone's advice. What if …? No, I won't think that – it's right. It's right.

"I can see the wheels turning, Lil, but don't second guess yourself. You've always had a good head on your shoulders and knowed how to make good decisions. I, for one, think it's the right one. Scott's a good man. Thomas and Maggie raised him right."

"Thanks, Mama. That means a lot to me." Lillian rose from the floor and stretched every muscle in her body and it felt good. She was slipping her shoes on when Lula stopped her.

"I've got some things – well, come on back and see." She led the way to her bedroom and motioned to the array of goodies on her side of the bed. "We should've done this sooner but, anyway, these are for your hope chest," she said proudly.

Lillian's jaw dropped and her eyes flooded with tears. She wrapped her arms around her mother and wouldn't let go. They stood that way for several minutes, more than likely recalling cherished memories of the time they had spent together over the past twenty years as mother and daughter, and friends.

Finally, Lillian pulled away and went to the bed to admire the pillow cases, towels, dish towels, and handkerchiefs, all embroidered either with hers and Scott's initials or birds and flowers. She dawdled over a set of dainty tea cups and saucers that she knew had belonged to her great-grandmother. How could they have remained intact all these years and how could anyone bear to give them away? "Oh Mama," was all she could manage. There were sheets and a beautiful blanket the color of the sky on a warm spring day.

Lula stepped over to the bed and picked up a quilt. "Lena helped me with this. She said she treasured the time you spent with her last year so she wanted something from that time on here." She moved her hand and there it was, down in the lower right corner, a mother hen with baby chicks embroidered into the green area of the quilt.

Lillian knelt beside her mother and laid her head on the quilt. So much love, so much trust, and yes, probably joy had come from the nimble fingers that created this exquisite work of art. All for me. And my husband. How could she ever thank them?

Lula, as usual, read her daughter's mind. "You can thank us by being happy, dear," she said. "Now, get up and stop your blubbering. You don't want to get all this stuff wet."

Lillian remained on her knees long enough to breathe a prayer of thanksgiving for all things.

Over the next year or so, family members came in their hit-and miss spare time, very seldom at the same time, but gradually the rocks and gigantic dirt clods were cleared from the garden space and the sheds went up almost like magic. Firewood to last the whole year was cut and stacked neatly against the back of the house. The spring was cleaned of leaves and debris that very well could have been there for decades. Pine trees close to the house had been sacrificed, but it was worth it with everything else that demanded their attention.

"Scott," Lillian cried into the darkness of the blistering hot August night. "It's time to get Doc Heacker. Hurry!" She bent double with the third contraction in the last half hour.

Scott was on his feet and dressed before she could straighten up. "Why didn't you say something, Lil?"

Through clenched teeth, Lillian reminded him that even if they notified the doctor he wouldn't come until the last minute. "Just get Mama," she begged. "She knew it was close so she's ready."

Scott disappeared into the night.

1926

By the time they had been through that ordeal three times, they felt like experts, and there, framed in the center of their hearts were the loves of their lives to show for it – Thomas Scott, Jr., Polke Alvin, and Armethia Daphne. Praise God from whom all blessings flow!

"Ain't she the prettiest thing you've ever seen?" Scott asked, easing the blanket back away from his daughter's face. Fifteen people agreed from the foot of the bed, then the doctor, suddenly realizing what was going on behind him, jumped up and herded them all toward the front door.

"Shoo! Shoo!" He slammed the door behind the last one. "I don't care if they are kin, they might be nasty." He literally washed his hands of the whole episode, assured Lillian and Scott he would be back in two days and took his leave.

What a memorable meeting it was when Junior and Polke were introduced to their little sister. Being three, and the oldest, Junior declared her his very own possession and made every endeavor to guide her steps where he wanted them to go until his dying day. She only complained once. Polke, the oh so close to a two-year-old, thought she was a new toy, therefore making her life miserable for the first few years.

One day Lillian thought she heard a scratching at the door, but unless Scott had brought home a dog, it had to be something else. Scritch-scratch! She took time to put the pan of biscuits into the oven then went to the back door. There stood a pitch-black hound dog, looking so mournful, so gloomy, so unpromising, maybe even depressed. Lillian couldn't seem to stop the barrage of words in her head describing this poor lost dog. Hungry came to mind so she grabbed a couple of biscuits from last night's supper and tossed them out the door.

Just then Scott appeared around the side of the house and yelled, "Hey, watch where you're throwing them rocks!" Junior came running right behind him, his arms outstretched to the dog.

Lillian was horrified. "Scott stop him. That dog might bite him!" She dashed out the door, tripped on the bottom step and lay there, face down in the dirt. The dog ran for dear life, Junior screamed and Scott laughed until he had to sit down, holding his aching sides. Finally, Lillian looked up. "I don't know what's going on," she said to her husband, "but since you are closer, you need to check on my "rocks" in the oven."

It was some time before she got herself cleaned up, Junior calmed down, supper served, Polke and Baby Metha bathed, fed and put to bed, and a cake baked before the fire went out for the night. Scott had retired to the rocking chair with Dog resting peacefully at his feet. At last Lillian whapped him on the back of the head, saying, "Get up. I gotta rock Junior for a few minutes."

In answer, Scott rose and ambled over to the cot by the door, motioning for Dog to follow, but he didn't.

After Lillian had told two stories and sung three songs, she carried the little boy to his bed in the back room, almost tripping over Dog on his way to join his young master. "Night, sweetheart," she said quietly.

"Night Mama. Night Daddy. Night Ole Foss." Junior patted the empty space on the little bed and Ole Foss hopped right up, turned around three times and lay down, as if he had been doing it all his short life. They never knew where the name came from but the bond that developed between the two was to be marveled at through the years. Ole Foss quickly blossomed into a beautiful, ebony prince and became a faithful companion to all in the family.

Scott slept on the little cot by the door for two whole nights because he couldn't stop laughing at the memory of his wife sprawled all over the back yard.

"Junior!" Lillian called, shading her eyes from the sun. She had spent more time looking for that child lately than doing her housework. He jumped out of bed every morning, full of life and curiosity and disappeared – either to watch Papaw Adcock work in the potatoes or scour every inch of the woods with Ole Foss. He always returned with his pockets full of treasure, forcing her to supervise the emptying ritual so Polke wouldn't be swallowing tiny pebbles, chewing on pine cones, or eating frog's legs.

Finally she caught a glimpse of his red cap at the edge of the garden and called again. "Junior, I need you in the house for a minute."

"What, Mama?" the little boy was always eager to please, if he would only be still long enough for her to enjoy him. She sat down at the round table and pulled him to her.

"Guess what?" Lillian's eyes twinkled. "Today is Daddy's birthday and we're having a party!"

"I like parties, Mama! Can it be in the woods? We could look for moss and bugs and …."

"Whoa, partner. No bugs!" Lillian laughed. She could hear Metha in the back room, screaming to be fed so she hurried and explained her plan. "Honey, what I need you to do is ask Daddy to play a game or two of marbles in the barn so he won't come in and see the cake and stuff until I'm ready. Okay?"

"I could tie him up and let Ole Foss guard him."

"No, sweetheart. Just play marbles." Poor Scott.

Later as people poured through the door and made themselves at home, Junior could be found on the back porch, emptying his pockets for Joe, Vernal and Franklin, Dewey's oldest son. It occurred to Lillian that these guys would make outstanding babysitters for an active three-year-old. She had tried her sisters but they couldn't keep up with him.

By now, a lot of the guests had ventured outside with their plates loaded with good home-cooked food. Lula and Lena had brought over fried chicken and biscuits so Lillian only had to make the gravy and roast the potatoes. Margaret brought green beans fresh from her garden. Lillian was so proud of Nead for volunteering to make slaw and everyone enjoyed Nancy's strawberry lemonade. Then there were fresh cucumbers, tomatoes and onions from Papaw Fry's garden. But the cake was Lillian's pride and joy because her daddy had helped her make it. Her heart had ached at the sight of his hands gently breaking the eggs because she knew how painful it was for him.

Now Scott came up behind her and whispered, "Great party, Lil." He turned her to face him. "How come I couldn't come in til it was almost over?"

Lillian's laughter rang throughout the house. "I put Junior in charge of you, then I forgot! I guess he did, too."

"Well, at least I got a piece of cake," he mumbled as he passed a tray of cheese and crackers to Sam and Nancy. "Here, sis, better grab some before they're gone."

"Where's that lovely little girl of yours?" Lillian asked Nancy as soon as she had caught her breath. "You did bring her, didn't you?" Helen and Metha were about the same age.

Nancy pointed toward the back room. "I put her down with Metha. It took a while to shoo Polke out, though." They laughed at the little boy's dedication to protecting his sister. "Hazel is in there with them in case he comes back!" Lillian knew they were in good hands with Dewey's wife in charge.

The crowd had gathered around the bonfire at the end of the yard. Darkness was falling fast so they let the fire die down to just colorful embers and began to collect their things and head home.

"Wait, wait!" Scott stood in the middle of the yard, pretending to cry.

"What's wrong, son?" Preacher Tyler asked in mock concern.

Scott wiped his eyes and announced in despair, "Nobody sung 'happy birthday' to me!"

Everyone looked at each other, then burst out laughing. Someone yelled out, "Lillian said not to sing until we were ready to leave!"

So they ended the party by singing 'happy birthday' while Scott chased his wife around the house, down the driveway, across the garden and into the barn where they landed on a soft bed of hay, arms entwined, smiling into each other's eyes.

1928

Two whole months had passed since they had found the body, planned the funeral, signed all the papers and laid their beloved William to rest in the Adcock family cemetery – husband, father, and friend, forever absent from their lives. Two whole months of suffering silently, suffering together. They could go several days without mentioning him at all then a word here or memory there or the familiar smell of someone's pipe would have them going over and over it again. Will his soul be lost? Did he really mean to drink the poison? How can we live with the embarrassment? Why didn't he trust us enough to tell us how bad the pain was? Why couldn't we see it for ourselves? What if someone had found him sooner?

On and on it went until it began to tear their family apart. Lena and others tried to help, but it was Lillian who spent more and more time with Lula. It was exhausting constantly trying to convince her that nobody was at fault, answering the same questions again and again. Scott spent his time doing the things at home that his wife would normally do. He resented every dirty dish, every unmade bed, and pushed the boys harder than ever before to do their chores and lessons for school. Add in a rambunctious two-year-old and it was almost overwhelming.

Finally, Lillian returned home to her own bed. That's where Scott found her one Tuesday night.

"You wouldn't listen to me, Scott. I tried to tell you and you wouldn't listen."

Scott hung his head. He had heard these same words for months now and his nerves were raw. "Okay, Lil, I take part of the blame – I thought maybe living with the constant pain of the Rheumatiz was affecting his mind. I didn't realize how serious it was"

"Of course you didn't," she mumbled into her pillow. "Why couldn't you see him going downhill? Even Mama can't tell you when it started, but I know the very day." She sat up in bed, her eyes pleading with him to understand how well she had known her Papa and how much it hurt that they had done nothing. "That very day ... I found him down at the spring, just sitting there."

Scott reached for her hand, but she scooted away from him. "Lillian, I saw him down there lots of times, just sitting there. Sometimes," he chuckled in spite of himself, "sometimes he'd be holding a frog or just a stick and be talking away. I didn't think anything was wrong. He was getting old."

"You interrupted me. I was going to say he didn't know me. He didn't know who I was, Scott! I talked to him and brought up every good memory I could think of and ... nothing. I told Mama about it and she said it had been happening for a long time but he always came around. Why didn't we do something?"

"You know how much pain he was in, Lil. Maybe it just got to be too much. Even the medicine Doc Heacker gave him had stopped working so what more could be done?"

"Doc Heacker!" Lillian practically spit the words out. "He could've give him something stronger that wouldn't have killed him. I don't know. I just don't know any more." She leaned back on the pillows again and patted the space beside her. "Come sit," she said quietly, "I'm not mad at you anymore."

Scott smiled and joined her on the bed. This time she let him hold her hand. "Just one more thought, Sweetheart." He looked into her eyes, but he could only see a reflection of himself. "Do you think there's any chance he might have drunk the stuff by mistake? You know, thinking it was something else?"

"No," a sweet little voice spoke from just inside the door. Junior stepped into the light of the kerosene lamp and faced his parents. "He knowed what he was doing," he said. Still a couple of months from his seventh birthday, he seemed much older.

"Come on in, son, and explain yourself. How would you know that?" Scott's voice was harsher than he intended, but he was dreading hearing what the little boy might have seen or heard. The old man had been spending a lot of time working with the potatoes, getting them ready to plant and Junior was his "big boy" helper.

Junior came to the side of the bed and Lillian lifted him up beside her. Hugging him tight and brushing the hair back off his forehead, she whispered, "Tell us what you know, Baby."

"Papaw was working with the potatoes next to the shed. He let me cut some of the eyes off of them 'cause his hands was hurting. Then he said he needed something to kill the bugs so he went into the shed."

Scott jumped up from the bed. "And left you there with a knife in your hand! How could he be so ....?"

"Scott! It's a little late to be worrying about that. Sit!" Lillian's voice was shaky, but she made her point. Scott sat down and waited for Junior to continue.

"Daddy, you teached me how to work with a knife. I was having fun!"

"You're right, son. Tell us the rest."

Junior drew in a deep breath. "When Papaw came out of the shed, he had this bottle that looked like medicine, so I asked him if it was medicine for the bugs and he laughed. He said, 'this stuff could kill a horse before you could say Jack Rabbit!'"

Scott and Lillian looked at each other over the boy's head. Their thoughts were the same, *he knew.*

Junior twisted away from his mother. "Mama, you're getting me all wet. Are you crying?"

"I guess so, but I'll stop." She wiped her eyes on the pillow case that her mother had embroidered for her a long time ago. "Did Papaw say anything else?" she asked quietly.

Junior nodded his head against his daddy's knee. "He said, 'tell 'em this pain is killing me.' Then he went into the shed again, and I followed him."

Lillian gasped and whispered, "Oh, no!"

"Did I do something wrong, Mama?"

"No, baby, no! You didn't."

Scott finally found his voice. "Junior, what did you see in the shed? What happened?"

"Papaw drunk the medicine, Daddy. All of it. Then he was all bent over and was holding his tummy and he said it again, 'tell 'em the pain is killing me' then he fell down and I went on to school."

"Whatever made you leave him, son?"

"It was the day for races and games outside, remember?" The big brown eyes darted back and forth between the two of them. "I should have gone to get Mamaw, shouldn't I?" Thinking that he might have been able to save his beloved Papaw was more than his little heart could bear. He rose up on his knees and clasped his mother's face in his hands. "I should have hid the medicine, Mama. I should have told Mamaw. I should've ...." Regret and grief that he had lived with for two dark months swallowed his baby words and he collapsed in his parents' comforting arms.

The three of them sat huddled in the middle of the bed, each with his own thoughts, each with his own tears. Maybe, with time, the horrors of the past few weeks could be erased from a little child's mind. All the love they could pour out onto his heart, all the attention they could possibly give him, all the prayers lifted to heaven on his behalf, maybe, with time, could heal the hurt.

Indeed, with the passing of time, life carried them along at its own pace. They weren't any wealthier, and their health had not improved enough that you could tell, but the sun seemed to shine a little brighter as memories faded. They could go about their business with a lighter step; the children no longer considered it a hardship to do their own chores and then skip down the way to help Mamaw Adcock with hers. Laughter rang out as they carried water, gathered firewood, and helped care for the farm animals. Polke found himself enjoying feeding the chickens and gathering eggs so it wasn't long until he convinced his parents to let him have his own. It also wasn't long until they became Metha's.

"Mama, she's doing it again!" Polke's tear-stained face peeked thru the outhouse door.

"Son, I'm busy. Go tell Daddy," Lillian said, sighing deeply. *When will I ever get a minute to myself?*

"I told Daddy and he said to tell you."

Figures. She finished her business and hurried back down the trail, Polke hustling to keep up. "Now, what is it?" Lillian asked, sitting on the back step and patting the space beside her.

Instead of sitting down, the little boy began to demonstrate his problem. "You see, I have my hens on this side of the barn." He laid out the area of the barn neatly in the air. "And she keeps moving them to this side and saying they're hers!" Again he made it plain that it was opposite sides of the barn. "Does that make them hers just cause she moves them?"

Lillian wasn't sure which bothered him most – the moving or the claiming possession. "No, that doesn't make them hers, but you know what we've always told you about sharing, hmm?"

"Yeah," he dug his toes into the dirt around the step. "If I give her one, will you make her stop?" He looked pleadingly into his mother's eyes.

"I tell you what," Lillian said, thinking on the spot. "You know Papaw's goat, Daisy?"

Polke nodded but already wondered what a goat had to do with chickens.

"Well," Lillian was happy to report, "she's going to have a little baby goat of her own any day now and when it is old enough, you could have it for a pet. Is that good?"

"Yes! Oh, Mama, I will love it and take care of it and ...." He suddenly ran out of words.

"You're thinking about your chickens, aren't you? How you might not have time to care for them and a baby goat too, huh?"

"Well," he finally sat down on the bottom step then continued, "if Metha just had chickens and didn't have a baby goat, she wouldn't have to move them around so much, you see."

So forever after, when people came to the farm, they were greeted by a billy goat, a rogue rooster, and 13 hens. And they always left with a dozen fresh eggs.

1934

God smiled again on this mountain family, adding joy and happiness to their lives with the births of their precious Hayes Edward and Glenneva Rozella (forever affectionately known as Jack and Cally).

"Mama, is Santy Claus real?" Two-year-old Jack had just learned to buckle his shoes and was practicing right in the middle of the bed. Lillian scooted him over and eased her pregnant body down beside him. "Child, this is September, a long way from Christmas. What made you think of Santa Claus?" Jack shrugged his shoulders and admitted he didn't know where the thought had come from. But he persisted. "Is he, Mama?"

Lillian knew she had a million things to do before the rest of the family came home but she looked into her little boy's big brown eyes and smiled. "You know, Jack, in a way, yes, Santa is real." And she began to tell him a story.

"It was the Christmas that I was eight years old, and we lived down the road from Plez and Dora Adcock. The county newspapers were encouraging children to write a letter to Santa so he would know for sure what they wanted."

"Did you write a letter, Mama?" Jack's eyes sparkled as he thought of what could happen if he wrote a letter to Santy Claus.

"Yes, Baby, I did. Mama helped me and that was okay 'cause she already knew what I wanted – a doll with open and shut eyes. I had seen one that the Adcock girls had and I came awfully close to coveting it."

"What's coveting – stealing? Would you steal it, Mama?" The little boy was shocked that his mama could even think of stealing something.

Lillian laughed and ruffled his nut-brown hair. "No, son. Coveting is wanting something so badly that you *might* steal it. It was just a feeling, not something I did. But this is a good time for you to listen carefully. If you're ever in a situation like that you come to me or Daddy and we'll discuss it, okay?" Jack agreed heartily and then urged her to finish the story.

"Well, Mama felt she had to read my letter before she wasted a stamp on it." Even now, Lillian giggled to herself at how crafty Lula had been. "Then she went down to visit with Minnie and Tilda and they agreed that they really were too old to play with dolls and then I found Maggie, that beautiful almost-new doll with open and shut eyes under our tree for Christmas!"

Jack buckled and unbuckled his shoes some more. He was anxious to show Junior and Polke not only that he could do it but how fast! "So, did Santy Claus bring you the doll?" he asked.

"I thought he did because of my letter but here's where you have to try hard to understand, son. What really happened was Mama read my letter and then made a deal with Minnie and Tilda and I got the doll. Now don't you think that's a nice way to get a gift?"

"Yes, Mama." Jack stretched out on the bed, thoughtfully considering his mother's story. "But that way," he said at last, sitting up and leaning against her swollen belly, "you didn't get to hear Rudolph on the roof!"

"Mama, tell us about when you saw the aeroplane land in a field," Junior wrapped the quilt a little tighter around his shoulders, juggling three-year-old Jack on his lap. He grinned at Lillian. They so very seldom had all the family together so now they gathered around the open grate, snug and warm, while Mama rocked and nursed baby Glenneva. Popcorn and crisp red apples were passed around.

Scott waved the children off. "Come on fellas. You've heard that story so many times …."

"But we like it, Daddy," Polke said. "She says it funny." He giggled just thinking about it.

"Well, as you know," Lillian began, "it was way back in 1920 right before your daddy and me got married. I was still living at home." Her eyes twinkled as she remembered. "Dewey and Hazel was already married but they lived with us for a while. So anyways, they asked me to go with them out to the Justice place in Wartburg to pick beans. There was lots of families in this county that would plant more garden truck than they could use so they'd let you come and pick whatever they had left." Lillian shifted the baby to the other breast amid moans from the boys.

"Well, there we were all bent over with our rears in the air just minding our own business. Hazel was singing "Swing Low, Sweet Chariot" at the top of her lungs when suddenly we heard this really loud, kinda weird noise and a great wind swept through." She paused to let everyone laugh because they knew what was coming next.

"Well, before we knew what was happening, our dresses blew up over our heads, and all three hats went tumbling out across the field. It was a sight to see. When we could finally look up there was this great big machine up in the air. How could that be? Did Mr. Justice's tractor get away from him?" The room rocked with the children's laughter because they had learned that she put a different question in there every time.

"Well, Hazel thought it was the Lord coming but Dewey shushed her and said, 'I never heard no cloud make *that* kinda noise!'" Lillian laughed at the memory.

"It's getting late, boys and girls," she said, carefully easing the sleeping infant onto the bed and trying to shoo the others out.

"No, Mama," Jack begged. "You gotta say the end to us!"

"Well," Lillian straightened her aching back. "Turns out it was a aeroplane – the owner had took off in Lexington, Kentucky and made it all the way to here. Then he run out of gas and had to drop down to earth like a bird. We like to never got that dust and dirt off ourselves."

"But you saved the beans, right?" Jr. asked, as he did every time.

Lillian grabbed her precious oldest son in a bear hug, squeezing oh so tightly. "You know we did, you little booger 'cause you eat 'em all!"

1936

It had been apparent for quite a while that Lillian needed to find work of some kind outside the farm. They had made a deal with Coalfield school to sell potatoes to them and Scott's pension had finally come through, but it was all a piddling amount in the face of their expenses.

As a division of the New Deal Agency, the W.P.A. (Works Progress Administration – later changed to Works Projects Administration) was still offering jobs to the "breadwinner" in the family.

In spite of her trepidation at leaving her children every day, Lillian was first in line at the courthouse in Wartburg the next week, practically the only woman there. She was assigned to a soup kitchen that had been set up a couple of miles from her house, for thirty hours a week and a minimum-wage-salary of $1.25 per hour, and, except for the trek back and forth in all manner of weather conditions, she was delighted. The group of women welcomed her and they became friends in a very short time.

The W.P.A. also set up a community garden at the school so Lillian and Scott made a deal that they would work there, harvest the produce, and can it "on the halves", meaning they would do all the work then return half to the school to be used in the soup kitchen. Round and round it went – "Cast thy bread upon the waters: for thou shalt find it after many days." Ecclesiastes 11:11 KJV

Lillian was in a tizzy. It was already past time to leave for the soup kitchen and none of the chores had been done. The baby needed to be fed, Jack and Ole Foss had scampered off with Metha's hair ribbons, sending her into a fit of anger, and the big boys were arguing over whose turn it was to get wood for the fire.

While it was all well and good that Scott had agreed to watch out for Metha and take care of Jack any time she had to work, he didn't seem to realize all the other things that needed to be done. He kept sending the two of them to school with ratty hair, wrinkled clothes and sometimes no lunch. Metha's teacher had even sent her home with a note saying, "Please wash this child's neck and ankles. They are rusty!" Lillian turned purple even now just thinking about it. She had determined to make Metha get her bath at night, complete with a shampoo, to avoid the endless rush in the mornings. But here she was again, fighting time.

She sat down to nurse the crying baby. "Metha, stop your yapping and get the comb. We'll do your hair before it dries," she called to her daughter, hoping it was loud enough to wake Scott. "I just can't seem to ever catch up," she mumbled, mostly to herself, a little bit to the baby. *And oh how I need a cup of coffee.* "Polke, it's your turn to get the wood!"

Scott suddenly came in the back door and plopped down into a chair. Lillian laughed in spite of herself. "I've been making all kinds of noise trying to get you out of bed! Where've you been?"

He waved her off. "I get so aggravated with your mother. I just can't help it. One of the cows got out and instead of sending Old Davy to fetch it, she sent him over here to get me!"

Lillian had lost interest as soon as she heard the word 'cows'. "Well, now that you're here, could you please make us some coffee?" She buttoned up her dress and carried the sleeping Cally back to the bedroom, gently placing her in the cradle Papaw Wiggins had made for Junior all those years ago. Scott came up behind her and playfully pushed her onto their bed, which, of course had not been made.

"Coffee's on. How about if we do double duty?" he asked, nuzzling his wife's neck.

Metha stood in the doorway with the comb. "What's double duty?" she wanted to know.

Scott sat up quickly and took the comb from her. "Well, it's like doing two things at once. Here, I'll show you. Hand me Mama's brush." Lillian poked him in the ribs and he meekly added, "Please?" He sat on the bed, leaning back against the headboard and instructed Lillian to sit in front of him. "Now, Little Bit, you sit in front of Mama." The little girl's eyes were shiny in the dim light.

"Oh, I get it!" she exclaimed, and they continued to brush and comb one hundred strokes each. Metha left the room with a parting shot of, "Mama, you got a brown mouth again."

"That little rascal!"

Scott wrapped his arms around Lillian and whispered in her ear, "You never mind her. I finally get it too, Sweetheart. I can do more than one thing at a time!"

Things wouldn't really calm down, though, until school was out and the kids could run freely and not worry so much about appearances. But for now, life was bearable even with Mama working.

One morning the first week in April, however, Scott came in from the garden to find Lillian packing her mother's old cardboard suitcase. He watched for a minute with neither of them speaking. She gently placed underwear, stockings, two dresses, a pair of house slippers, and a package of what he knew to be homemade cookies into the case, closed the lid and snapped the locks. When she looked up at him, he was grinning.

"Whew! Is that all you're taking? I thought you were packing up everything and leaving me!" He gathered her in his arms and kissed her gently. "You wouldn't leave me, would you?"

"Yes, Scott," she said solemnly, "I am leaving you."

"But, but ..." he sputtered, "I wouldn't last five minutes without you! How will I ever -?"

Lillian interrupted him. "I would laugh at you but then I'd start crying." She pulled away from him and sat in the rocking chair, fingering the cobalt blue feather on the hat she had chosen to take with her. "It will be longer than five minutes, but I won't be too far away. Mama, Margaret and I are going to stay a few days with Aunt Lena. Charles has made all the arrangements for us to take her to the doctor."

"Sounds like he's afraid of what they might find, huh?"

"Well, with blood pressure that high you have to be concerned with strokes and she's just as stubborn as Mama when it comes to doctors and hospitals."

"What about the soup kitchen?" Scott asked. "They need you, too."

"Gladys is taking my place," she answered rather sharply, then reassured him, "I'll do something nice for her when I get the chance. She knows."

"So, did you make me out a list of where everything is and what has to be done?"

She punched him on the shoulder and motioned for him to pick up the suitcase. "Don't be silly, dear. Of course I did!" They left the room hand-in-hand, knowing their time before she left was precious.

They both walked out of the holler with the children the next morning, where Lillian would catch her ride at the top of the hill. The whole family had sighed with relief when she had announced that she was taking the baby with her. Jack's brown eyes twinkled as he assured her he'd had no plans to drown his sister in the spring, but he was glad he didn't have to feed her. "I've never seen such a messy eater!" he exclaimed as he picked up shiny rocks and stuffed them in his pocket.

"Come along, son," Scott called, "it's time for us big boys to head back home." He winked at Junior and Polke, knowing they considered themselves grown-ups with real jobs. He took Jack's little hand in his own and, as they turned back down the hill, informed him that he had been a messy baby, too. "I remember one morning …."

Jack snatched his hand away and covered both ears. "Don't tell that one again, please Daddy?"

Scott agreed then glanced back to get one more look at his wife and bid her and Metha a good day, but they were all out of sight.

He walked slowly, letting the April sunshine warm his aching back as he prayed for his family's safety and Lena's healing.

But the earthly healing was not to be. The "three musketeers" as Scott had labeled them had returned home to their families and Lena was left in the care of her children and loving husband. The blood pressure had been diagnosed as malignant and she had developed pneumonia, so it was no surprise when word came of her death. Lula was not up to attending the services so Scott took Cally to her house to keep her company. "At least the sun is shining," he whispered to himself.

They laid their precious wife, sister, aunt, and friend, Lena Mae Fry Clark to rest in the Davis Cemetery. Everyone should have an Aunt Lena.

Heartbreak has many faces and has a way of affecting generation after generation. Death, lost loves, or precious lives headed for destruction.

"Lillian, he ain't coming in this house like that. Think of the young 'uns."

"Well, he ain't sleeping on the porch either. Help me move that cot over here closer to the door then you go on back to bed. I'll take care of this."

With tears flowing, she helped her oldest son stumble through the door and watched as he sprawled onto the cot, filthy clothes and all, drunk as the proverbial dog. For awhile he giggled like the little boy that he was, then the tears swallowed him up, then finally the sickness. "Oh, Mama, I feel so bad."

"Shush, boy. We'll talk about that later." Lillian brought a pan of cold water and bathed his face and hands. She tried taking off the nasty flannel shirt but he held tight. Blessed sleep came to him at last and she slowly made her way back to bed.

"How's he doing?" Scott asked, reaching for her in the darkness. Words and scalding tears choked her but she managed to assure him that their son would recover.

"Maybe it's just this one time, you know, somebody dared him or something."

But her wishful thinking was for naught. Junior continued to drink and stagger in home and Mama continued to clean him up, get him back on his feet so he could do it all over again.

That first morning Polke had discovered his older brother on the cot and was told the story. Metha had come in later and remarked at the sickening smell and the deathly look on her brother's face. Parents can only explain so much so she and Polke had cornered Junior later when he was sober and insisted on some answers. He had been adamant that, "Everybody does it," and "It makes me feel better."

"Well, it doesn't make Mama and Daddy feel better so stop it," Metha had declared, hands on her hips and her brown eyes flashing. "You know better, Junior!"

Polke had found his answers and decided he'd like a taste of the good stuff so he joined his brother on his escapades. Lillian was more resentful of the process with this addition so Polke learned to clean himself up before he reached home but it was still a part of their daily lives, with Jack and Cally living in the shadows.

1937

Lillian leaned against the door of the shed, watching Scott clean William's garden tools. "Almost ten years now," she murmured.

"I know, Lil. I think of him, too. He was a good man."

"I'm glad to hear you say that, Scott. I've heard remarks in the Switch that he was crazy, selfish to leave Mama like that, maybe even go to hell."

"Don't pay no attention to that, Honey. We come to terms with that a long time ago."

"I know," Lillian said, leaning to kiss him on the cheek. "That's not what I wanted to talk to you about anyway."

"Hit me."

Lillian shivered and pulled her coat tighter around her body. Summer had come and gone with hardly a 'howdy-do' as her grandmother Martha would say. "It's Mama. She's sick."

"I know that, Lillian. She's had that ulcer now for months and she's tired all the time. The boys and I have been doing her heavy work around the house for a long time." He stopped himself before she got the idea he was complaining. And then he remembered Dewey and Hazel had come yesterday to take Lula to the doctor. "There's something else?"

Lillian covered the distance between them in two steps and he wrapped her in his arms and waited for the tears to abate. "Let's go on home, hon. It's a little nippy out here." Moving as quickly as possible,

Scott put away the tools and cleaning supplies. Lillian handed him the bow saw and they were finished.

"What did Doc Heacker say?" Scott asked as soon as he had a cup of coffee in his hand. He eased his aching body down into the rocking chair and motioned Lillian to sit on his lap but not spill the hot drink.

Her smile was weak but she sat carefully, glancing around to make sure none of the kids were within earshot. "They didn't take her to Heacker. They went to Dr. Stone in Oliver Springs."

"The new guy? What did he say?"

"It's called phthisis (tie-sis), or consumption or tuberculosis or whatever they're calling it these days." She drew in a deep breath. "And she has that influenza stuff that's going around."

"So that's what's causing the fever and chills?"

"Well, it all works together is what Dewey said." Lillian rose from Scott's lap and left the room. He found her a few minutes later on the tiny back porch and convinced her to do her crying in the warmth of the kitchen.

They sat together at the table until she was ready to continue. "Oh Scott. I just can't lose anybody else! It's too hard." She put her head down on the table and wept as though her heart would break. At last the ugly words came out. "There's a brain abscess that's complicating things."

"A what?"

"I don't know any more than that."

"So," it pained him to ask, but he needed to know. "Is this tie-sis thing contagious?"

"Whether it is or not, we have to be careful." She felt cold even in the heat of the kitchen. "You know Gladys has been staying over there with her at night."

They decided not to spend precious time on maybes and what-ifs. In the next few weeks Lula's children and their families made decisions they never thought they would have to make. There were the household and farm chores to consider and medical bills to deal with, but the one that tugged at their heartstrings was determining where and how Lula would spend her last days. In the end, it wasn't for them to decide.

"Evan, I don't care what any of you say I'm not going to no sanitarium. If I'm gonna die, I'll die right here at home in my own bed." Then with a rare grin she added, "Well, maybe the hospital."

So the days blended with the nights with people covering shifts so that she was never alone and never wanted for anything. They each, right down to the youngest, knew and followed, the safety precautions the doctor had outlined. The farm continued to prosper with produce for all who tended it, and, much to Lula's chagrin, the house had never been cleaner.

One dark, gloomy evening toward the end of January, Lillian sat beside her mother's bed, keeping her hands busy making a flour-sack dress for Cally, but her heart just wasn't in it. Setting her things aside, she whispered, "Mama?"

There was no answer but there really hadn't been any response for several days. "It's snowing, Mama," Lillian continued. "Maybe tomorrow we can go up to the Camp and sled down the hillside like we used to, you think?" *Don't leave me!*

Suddenly Lula sat straight up in bed and looked around the room, her eyes lingering on the old furniture, the closet door with the kids' heights marked on it, and then Lillian. "I had a good life, you know."

Lillian could only nod.

Lula eased back onto the pillows again and seemed to be sleeping peacefully. "You know I love you, don't you, Mama?" Lillian whispered, thinking only she could hear.

"Yes, child. I know." The voice was weak, but for a few precious moments for Lillian, the mind was clear.

Then she heard, "Tell William – tell William," and finally on the third try, "Tell William I forgive him."

It was a wintry, bitterly cold day when they laid their treasured mother, mamaw, sister, aunt, and friend, Lula Frances Fry Adcock, to rest in the Adcock family cemetery. Our hearts are broken.

1938

One evening, when Junior was getting dressed to go out, he glanced through the bedroom window and saw Lillian relaxing in the swing on the front porch. "Oh boy," he said under his breath. "Guess I'll have to go out the back door." Making sure every shiny, coal-black hair was in place and his white shirt was tucked in just so, he crossed the living room into the kitchen and reached for the backdoor knob.

No surprise here – Scott was sitting on the back steps, casually sipping his last cup of coffee of the day and studying the stars flickering across the sky. "Going somewhere, son?" he asked, as if he didn't know the answer. He patted the top step, inviting Junior to have a seat, which he reluctantly did. They heard footsteps approaching from the front yard and Lillian magically appeared and settled herself on the second step.

"Okay," the boy mumbled, "whadya want now?"

Lillian chuckled. "Honey, if I had what I wanted, you'd be about three years old again and I could control you with a dirty look."

Scott poked her shoulder. "Good one, Mama!" He set his cup down and stretched his legs out around his wife. "What we want son, is to find out who's leading you astray." He held up his hand to ward off any denial then continued. "We've let this go on far too long. Who were you supposed to meet tonight, and now you're not?"

Junior snorted loudly. "I'm not …."

"Yes, you are. Give me a name."

Hearing the sternness in his father's voice, Junior knew he had to give in. "Billy. Billy Harris."

Lillian gasped and dropped her head onto her arms. *Really? Corrie's little Billy? Golden Boy?*

"There has to be a story with that," she said quietly. "Talk."

Junior drew in a ragged breath and related what he knew. "He grew up around here but he ain't got no daddy. Not a real one anyway." He glanced at his father, trying to relate that he knew what a real daddy was. "His mother got married again and made him move up north somewhere. Michigan, I think. Then last year, she and Billy moved back here – they're over in the old Adkisson place and, well, he was already drinking, making his own stuff and," here he took another deep breath, "selling it."

Lillian was numb. "Where on earth do you get money to buy anything?"

"Mamaw give me and Polke some of Papaw's stuff and ...."

"And what?" Scott yelled so loud it scared the other two. "And what, Junior? Please don't tell me that you sold your Papaw's things? Swapped them? Bartered them? What?"

Junior rose and took a few steps toward the front yard. When he turned back, he was crying. "It was just some old saws and Billy said let him have 'em and he knew where he could sell them. After I had that one drink, I was hooked. I couldn't quit. But it was a good feeling, making the deal, then drinking the stuff. I felt grown up."

Scott stood up, too. He would have towered over his son but the pain from his injuries had caused him to stoop his once stately frame. Now they were eye-to-eye in the semi darkness. "This is beside the point we started discussing, but, by rights, the saws you took, old or not, belong to your mother and her brothers and sisters. Your grandmother was wrong to give them away, especially without asking." He looked at Lillian and she shook her head.

"I don't care about that right now, Junior," she said. "I want to know what you are going to do to get over this, this drinking problem."

"Look, son, a lot of men around here drink – they all have their reasons. I like a drink now and then myself, but we don't want you doing it. And I'm really disappointed that you dragged your little brother into it."

"He didn't drag him, Scott."

Scott exploded. "See there? See there? You always defend him!"

Lillian remained remarkably calm. "I know Billy's mother. I'll talk to her."

Now it was Junior's turn to blow. "You can't do that, woman! They'll laugh me outta Coalfield! I'm past fifteen years old – I can make my own decisions."

Scott had weakened after his outburst. "Don't talk to your mother like that, son," he said, without conviction. "Let's get some sleep and talk about this tomorrow." He and Lillian disappeared into the house, stopping to check on their other children, then crawling into bed, exhausted from the confrontation more than their day's work.

Later that night, actually in the wee hours of the morning, Lillian heard the boys' bedroom window slide open and the thunk of boots on the floor, but she couldn't be sure if someone was coming or going. Sleep overtook her as she visualized baby Billy, so innocent then, so deadly now.

"Corrie, I did," Lillian was insisting. "I even sent Mama over there and Adele implied that you had died. When she finally admitted that you had moved up north, I tried to get an address but she said she hadn't heard from you." Lillian ran out of breath.

"Well, most of it is true," Corrie said. They sat side-by-side in the porch swing at Corrie's "new" house. She had been so lonely and spent a good bit of time thinking about visiting Lillian but always lost her nerve. Everybody had their own lives these days and didn't want old schoolmates popping in. She sweetened her tea with two cubes of sugar then set the cup down. "She kicked me and Billy out when I told her I was marrying Johnny Monroe so I didn't let her know where we was. Some people don't deserve to be parents."

Lillian agreed inwardly but wasn't in the mood to discuss Adele Whitaker. She leaned back and let Corrie control the speed of the swing. Finally, taking a sip of her tea, she stated the purpose of her visit. "I came to talk about what Billy is doing."

Corrie didn't even ask what she meant. "What Billy is doing? What about what Junior Wiggins is doing? He is your son, isn't he?" Corrie's voice rose with each word.

Lillian sighed and set her tea cup back on a little side table. This so-called friendship was about to be tested beyond measure. "Yes, he is," she answered calmly. "What is it you think he is doing?" She started to emphasize the word 'think' but decided to hold her tongue until the story was out. She also wished Scott had come along for moral support.

"He and his brother are the ones that built that still," Corrie declared. A smile of satisfaction twisted her lips when she caught Lillian's look of amazement. "Yeah, take that and chew on it!" Then suddenly realizing how she would feel if the tables were turned, she softened her tone. "I knew Billy was drinking before we ever left here. Then it just got worse in Michigan because … because he drank with John. When I figured out what was happening, I left John and brought Billy back down here. Little good that did." She turned to face Lillian in the swing. "Lillian, I swear, that moonshine still was already there. Billy didn't even know what it was."

Lillian stood and began pacing across the porch. Throwing her hands out in a helpless gesture, she said in an almost pleading voice, "That doesn't mean my boys did it." But even as she said the words, she had to accept that it was possible. They had other friends, other means of getting the materials. Junior had said they got the saws from Mamaw – maybe they got more than that. She stopped mid-step and leaned her head against the frame of the screen door and sobbed.

Corrie hesitated a few seconds then went to her friend and wrapped her in comforting arms. She whispered, "I was going to say 'I'm sorry' but I was afraid you might hit me!" They both laughed as they remembered another conversation a lifetime ago.

"I should go," Lillian managed to say through her tears. "I'll see what I can do about this, uh, situation. If I can get a hold on my feelings by the time I get home." She dried her face with the corner of her apron then looked at Corrie and smiled. "Friends?"

"Forever," Corrie said quietly.

Scott met Lillian at the back door. "Baby, I was starting to worry. I knew I should have gone with you." He reached for her hand and gently led her to the round table. Pulling out a chair for her, he asked, "Coffee?"

She declined the coffee but sat quietly waiting for him.

"Well?"

"He lied to us, Scott. He lied about the whole thing. Blaming Billy when it was really him and Polke."

Scott was on his feet, fuming. "You believed her? You believed things like that about our boys? How could you?"

"She was telling the truth, Scott. We should have asked Polke. At least he's babyish enough to let it slip."

"If, and I mean if, I find out that they did this and then one of them blamed somebody else," Scott said, shaking his head, and biting his tongue in anger. "I'll tear up their hides. They won't be able to sit down for a week!"

Lillian shook her head too, but with determination. "I won't let you do that, husband. They're just little boys. You can't do that."

"Lil, what kind of men do you think they're going to turn out to be if we don't take care of things now?" Scott drained his cup and came to stand behind Lillian's chair. "You think about it and we'll decide what has to be done after we talk to them. It's been a long day. I'm going to bed." By the time he had climbed the stairs, undressed and crawled into bed, he had forgotten what the conversation was about.

The boys, all of them, including Billy Harris, became men and continued their illicit foraging for materials to build as many moonshine stills as they deemed necessary for their entertainment. Nighttime was their friend with early risings, gainful employment, and family support taking a back seat.

Mama wept, but, as most have experienced, the tears were more for her own comfort than the building blocks of young lives.

1940

"Mama, hurry up. Me and Daddy are tired of waiting for you!" Five-year-old Cally was already out at the end of the yard, loaded down with a blanket and a jug of lemonade.

"You watch your mouth, young lady," Lillian called from the back door. "If Daddy had helped with this food, we'd already be there!" She gathered up the sandwiches, cookies, pickles, and Jack's favorite, little sausages on toothpicks, and crammed it all into a cardboard box. "Cally, sit down and rest a minute while I change my shoes. Where's Junior?"

Cally sighed as she plopped to the ground on top of the blanket. "Old Foss didn't come home last night so he went looking for him. He said to go on without him if he was late." She picked a daisy from the flower bed under the maple tree and started plucking petals – he loves me, he loves me not, he loves me, ….

"Okay, I'm ready," Lillian said. "Where's Jack?"

"Him and Polke are playing horseshoes with Daddy behind the barn," Cally answered. She seemed to have a bead on everybody's whereabouts which came in handy sometimes.

Just for fun Lillian asked, "Where's Cousin Oscar?"

"He came over to borrow a post hole digger and I told him about the picnic and asked him if he wanted to go and he said he would really like to but he had to fix a sexton of the fence so I said that's okay, we'll just go on without you."

Lillian was laughing out loud by the time the girl finished. Now she knew where everyone was but didn't have the energy to explain the difference between a sexton and a section.

Metha was pacing, actually counting off paces on the playground while waiting for her family. They should have been at the school thirty minutes ago. She hurried over to the principal. "Miss Lexie, they will be here. I know they will. They were so excited when I told them we were having a picnic to celebrate completing the eighth grade. Mama said it's been a long, hard journey and somebody better celebrate, so I know they'll be here. Can we wait a few more minutes?"

Miss Lexie smiled. "We'll wait ten more then we have to start or we won't have time for all the games."

Just then someone announced to the world that the Wiggins family was finally coming up the road. Everybody cheered, Metha blushed profusely, and Miss Lexie blew her whistle and shouted, "Let's get this show on the road!"

Thus eighth grade ended and hopes for the future began.

"There now," Metha said to herself, hanging the mop and broom on nails on the wall, "I won't have to do that again for a while." She had just finished cleaning Aunt Grace's house and was ready to leave when she heard someone call her name. Aunt Grace had gone to help Uncle Evan at their grocery store and the girl wasn't expecting her back so soon.

"Metha? Where are you?" Metha recognized her cousin Mildred's voice and went through the kitchen, living room and all the way to the high front porch before she found her. Determined not to be embarrassed by her cleaning garb, she smiled as she put on her ragged coat and gloves.

"I was just leaving. You can tell Aunt Grace I'll be back again next week. It's nice of her to help me earn money for school." She started to walk away but Mildred stopped her.

"That's what I wanted to talk to you about," she said, leading the way back into the house. "We heard about all the work you've been doing to earn money and this is the only way I could think of to help." She paused and leaned against the bedroom door. "See, I have some dresses that I've outgrown and Mama said they would dry rot if we waited for my sisters to grow into them and I don't think Herman would wear them." She laughed at her own joke. "Anyway, there's three of them plus some other stuff if you want it. I brought them up here to save you a trip out to my house." She waved a hand toward the bed, encouraging Metha to take a look.

"Mildred, I don't know what to say. I mean, not only helping me earn money for school, but a beautiful wardrobe, too?" Tears filled her eyes but she brushed them away with the scraggly gloves on her dishpan hands. At first she was awed by the generous offer, then embarrassed because she could give nothing in return, then elated that Mama wouldn't have to sew flour sacks. She gently caressed the hem of one of the dresses.

"That was my favorite," Mildred said in a low voice. "I'd be happy if you would take them."

"Thank you," Metha used the same whispery voice, almost as if the whole thing was a secret. The "other stuff" turned out to be a pair of sturdy black shoes that would fit with a little something stuffed in the toes, a pair of warm, fake-fur-lined gloves, three pairs of socks, and a navy blue hat that made them both laugh because it was Aunt Grace's.

1942

Everyone had declared it the best Christmas ever with friends and family crowded around the best ever Christmas tree, sipping hot chocolate and munching on homemade, hand-decorated cookies. Someone had even brought a big box of chocolate-covered cherries, which Jack promptly hid under his bed, hoping for a midnight snack, which Cally happened to find while searching for her bouncy ball that really bounced. Needless to say, Jack didn't get any cherries.

The stockings were emptied, folded flat and packed away, along with every scrap of wrapping paper and ribbon that could be salvaged. Metha had wanted the magnificent tree carried out to the back yard for the birds to enjoy the strings of popcorn and berries still clinging to its branches, but because of the six inches of snow on the ground and more expected, Scott said it would be just fine on the back porch. Really hungry birds would manage to find it.

It was Lillian's idea to have a quiet evening now, sprawled out over the house, writing their New Year's resolutions in secret. At first the older boys flat-out refused to write anything but finally Junior, chewing on the nub of a pencil he had borrowed from Cally, scribbled something then declared he was never doing it again. Polke could only find a crayon so his note was bigger than the others'.

They gathered at the round table, placed their slips of paper in Lillian's special box, watched her close and lock it, then made their way to bed, one by one.

In the shadows of midnight, someone was overcome with curiosity, opened the special box and read:

Scott – to join the Seventh-day Adventist church

Lillian – to be a better wife and mother

Junior – marry Evaleen Moore

Polke – have a family like ours

Metha – be a nurse so I can help people, be a good daughter and sister, read more, learn to cook better

Jack – quit school but Mama and Daddy would kill me so I guess I'll say be a soldyer like Daddy

Cally – grow up to be a teecher, and a mama and have lots of kids and pets and flowers at my house.

"Scott!" Lillian leaned out the bedroom window to call her husband. He waved to show her he had heard and started toward the house. The garden was never in good enough shape for him so any spare time he had was spent there. It was the family joke that they always knew where to find Daddy. He stopped to put away his tools and dust off his clothes before going inside. Lillian never fussed at him for messing up her clean house but he tried hard to respect her wishes – garden boots stay outside on the stoop!

"Hey hon, any coffee left?" He slipped his arm around his wife and kissed her lightly on the cheek.

"Plenty," she said, and turned to pour him a cup. "Sit. We need to talk."

"About what?"

"About letting our daughter go all the way to North Carolina to that Pisgah school. I'm still not sure I want her to go, especially so far. And you've never really agreed to it." She took a sip of his coffee. "By the way, I hate that name."

"Armethia? I thought you loved it."

She slapped him on the arm, making his drink slosh onto his leg. "Not *her* name – yours. I wish people would call you by your right name."

"Oh that again." He dismissed her with a smirk. "Maybe I don't like your name either, Lillian B. – what's the B for anyway?"

"All these years and you're just now asking?"

"I've asked you before. You just chose not to answer." Their laughter had a slight echo in the unusually quiet house.

"She's bent on going, Scott, so what else can we do? Everything is already lined up – a ride to the school, decent clothes, a good job waiting. You have to admit she worked hard after graduating high school and everything."

"I know but, you think they're good people – treat her right?"

"I don't see why not. It's Adventists – they're supposed to be the kindest people on earth. So you want to tell her she's going?"

Scott grinned and reached for her hand. "What did you need me here for, LB? You decided weeks ago, didn't you?"

Dear daughter,

Hope this finds you well. You never did tell us your room number but I guess they can find you easy enough. We are fine here – the usual aches and pains. Bonnie June is the sweetest thing. If I didn't know better, I'd think she misses you. I used all them flour sacks to make her some little dresses. She sure is crazy about her papaw. When Junior and Evaleen stop by to see us, she crawls to Scott as fast as she can on them chubby little legs – it's a sight to see. Jack won a spelling contest in his class so next time he will be up against the older class. Miss Jeffers said he could win a book by Beatrice Potter called The Tale of Peter Rabbit. He does love rabbits. Your daddy went hunting yesterday with Polke and Junior. They didn't shoot nothing but Scott said it was nice being with the boys, as he calls them, and Old Foss. Junior sure loves his dog. I just wish he would take better care of him. We had ice cream for my birthday. Who wants to celebrate getting old? HaHa Well, dirty clothes don't wash theirselves so I will close for now. Write back when you can. Love, your old Mama. PS. This bleeding is getting the best of me. I can't remember ever being so tired. I'll see what Doc Heacker says next week.

Dear Mama, Daddy, Junior, Evaleen, Bonnie June, Polke, Mabel, Jack, Cally and Old Foss,

Got your letter but hardly had time to read it, what with all the other stuff I have to do. Hope you all had a good Thanksgiving and a Merry Christmas. Cafeteria food is not so good, even on holidays. How's Cally? She must be awfully scared at school. I'm glad Daddy went hunting with the boys. Guess the wild animals are happy! I'm so glad about Jack – he always was good at his lessons and I know how much he loves rabbits. Hope you got all the clothes washed for everybody. I have to wash some of mine out the night before, especially the under things but I'm not complaining. I know you and Daddy do all you can to help me. Oh, yeah, what did Doc Heacker say about the bleeding? Write me again and tell everyone else to put a note in. Cally can draw a picture. Love to all, Metha. PS. I was going to surprise you and come home for a week but I got a new job and had to start right away. That sound you hear is me crying! Kiss Bonnie June for me. PSS. Mama, did you quit the you-know-what yet? Just wondering. Oh yeah – Happy New Year!

1943

Dear Metha,

Finally received your letter. Glad you found the time to write, what with all you have to do. I forgot to tell the kids to write a note so you'll have to wait till next time. Evaleen brought the baby over again today. She's eight months old now – still a chubby little thing - coming up on her first birthday before you know it. We thought sure her and Evaleen together would make Junior quit drinking but it don't look like it. She's a good person, though. Polke and Mable still don't have any kids. Hope they's nothing wrong. Do you remember her? James Carter's girl? They get along good. Your daddy sure is hateful these days but it's mostly my fault cause I stay so tired all the time and can't keep the housework up. It's all I can do to get to the soup kitchen every day. Jack helps a little but he likes to play, too. Doc Heacker says to just wait and see for a couple more months then he might send me to see Doc Bowman in Harriman. Hope you're not working too hard there at that place. It wears your body down. Love, Mama.

"Come on, Jack, we're going to be late again and you know what Mama will do," Cally said nervously. She always enjoyed stopping at the Little Emory creek on the way home from school, especially on a warm spring day, but also dreaded the whippings they got if they didn't go straight home. No matter how many times they tried to tell Mama how much fun it was to stick their toes into the cool water, search along the banks for frogs, and try to skip rocks on the top of the water, she simply didn't want to hear it.

Jack grinned at his sister and bent down to place the crawfish gently back into the water, whooping with delight as it skittered backwards in the muddy water and disappeared under a rock.

They managed to get their socks and shoes back on in record time and took off at a run. Maybe they could sneak in and Mama would never know. Cally suddenly stumbled and fell into the grass growing alongside the road. At first Jack thought it was funny, then realizing she might be hurt, he walked over and offered her a hand up. When they looked up, there was Mama, coming to meet them. Cally's heart sank. Why did I stop? It wasn't worth it just to see an old crawfish. She started to cry right there on the road.

Their mother's voice carried up and down the road and she couldn't seem to control the venom in her words or tone. Jack suddenly felt the need to run to the bathroom.

"If I've told you once, I've told you a thousand times to come straight home from school. You have work to do and your lessons to catch up on. I'm tired of saying the same thing over and over. Just wait til I get you home." Cally figured she would hear those words bouncing around inside her head for the rest of her life.

When all was said and done, Daddy held her on his lap and gently rubbed her aching legs until she fell asleep. "My poor little Rosebud," he murmured over and over, kissing the top of her head.

Jack found solace at the spring, wading in the cool water, kicking up the rotting leaves just the way his mother had done so long ago. It occurred to him that it just wasn't worth going to school if he had to pay such a price.

It wasn't many weeks later that school dismissed early and Jack and Cally were in seventh heaven. A whole afternoon of playing in the creek, maybe even visiting some cousins to play ball! They had just begun to take off their shoes and socks when a familiar form came to the top of the hill and turned right. We're not even late! Cally's heart cried.

This time, when the worst of it was over, Daddy had something to say. "Lillian, I've set back and watched this go on far too long and I want it stopped. These kids ain't done nothing but try to be kids." He reached for the switch and flung it across the room. Even though the children were in no shape to gloat, they did feel a little better. But then, there are always more switches to be found.

It wasn't many weeks later that Jack and Cally got up early on a Saturday morning, fixed their own breakfast, and set off around the ridge to visit Evaleen and the baby, stopping along the way to pick wildflowers and blackberries to share. They just hoped Junior wasn't there cause he would make them go straight back home.

The Moores lived in a log cabin, and that, of course, fascinated Jack. He also loved the mule that their son used to plow the garden. But what Cally was happiest about was getting to cook on the big cook stove. When they had gone before, Evaleen managed to find an apron that would fit the little girl and helped her wiggle into it, then they made a pie or biscuits or cornbread. Today they made biscuits and Mr. and Mrs. Moore sat with them at the long oak table, enjoying the delicious bread with honey and freshly churned butter. It was the perfect Saturday morning snack. Later, Mr. Moore let Cally help him gather eggs and pick up apples that had fallen the night before.

When the children deemed it time to leave, Evaleen helped them gather their treasures, and walked them to the end of the yard.

"I'm sorry Bonnie June slept the whole time you were here," she told them, just as if they were grownups who had come to visit.

"I could've waked her up real easy," Jack said with a grin. "I could even go now and –"

Evaleen caught him before he could even turn around. "Whoa!" she said. "Let's wait until next time you come and I'll see what I can do!" She gently pushed him in the direction of home. "Be sure and tell your mother I said hello," she said.

"Uh, I don't think we should do that." Jack said quietly.

"Why not, sweetheart? She's my friend."

"Well, we sorta didn't tell her we was coming here." He suddenly realized the enormity of what they had done and started to cry, which, of course, made Cally cry.

How stupid of me! Why didn't I ask? Evaleen ran back inside to tell her parents where she was going, grabbed a few of the biscuits, stuffed them in a bag and went back to the children. "I will walk home with you," she said. "Maybe you won't be in trouble."

But there would be no saving Jack and Cally. They spent the rest of the week wishing they had stayed in bed that Saturday morning, but Evaleen became a life-long, trusted friend.

Dear Metha,

Well, I reckon Bonnie June's birthday party is going to have to be a few days early cause Doc Bowman says if I don't have surgery, I'm going to die so I have to do what he says. They want me in the hospital on the 15th so I don't guess you can get here by then. Don't worry yourself over it. Anyways, I plan to perk up and enjoy that little girl as much as I can. Jack says to tell you he misses you. And your daddy does too. Bye for now, your old Mama

Mama,

Don't you dare have any surgery before I can get there! My supervisor says if I can get a ride I can come if you do need surgery but don't do anything till I'm there, okay? Tell Daddy and Polke and Jack and Cally and Junior and Evaleen and Bonnie June I said hello. Yeah, Mable wrote me a note last month. Said she was bored just sitting around! Her and Evaleen was always nice to the kids. I'm writing this during class and hope I don't get in trouble. It's so close to the end of the school year. Do you think we could arrange for me to come back next year? Just thinking out loud. Write me soon. Bye, your loving daughter.

Dear Metha,

This is your old dad. Hope all is well with you. We are fine here. Well, not really 'cause your mama just couldn't seem to get better so Doc Heacker and Doc Bowman both said don't wait for the 15th or she might die. Didn't you get Mama's last letter? May be lost somewhere. Anyway, her family didn't think she was strong enough to go through something like that, but you pretty much have to do what the doctors say. I hope they don't blame me with it. I stayed at the hospital with her for two nights. Just about killed me. Left Jack and Glenneva at your Aunt Nancy's. They send their love. Mama, too. Bye for now. PS - Is there any chance you could come on home?

Metha was exhausted. She had not slept well for several nights. Mrs. Wilson kept telling her to go to sleep now that they were on the road but all she could think about was how things were at home. What if she was too late? How do you go on without your mother?

Her supervisor had been kind enough to make all the arrangements for the trip home, and now she pulled the car up to the back door of the small home and helped Metha collect her things. "I'll be at my cousin's until Monday," she said quietly. "Just send word if you need to ride back with me, okay?"

The young girl shook her head and swiped at the tears with her sleeve. "I won't be going back, Mrs. Wilson. However this turns out, I won't be going back." She gave a slight wave, turned and made her way through the heavy door. Going directly to her mother's room, she crept in quietly.

In the weeks that followed, the sorrow and heartache went where they went, never easing for a moment, even in sleep. Cally was having nightmares practically every night. Metha would crawl into the tiny bed and coax her back to sleep, then at daylight, ease out of the house to do the outdoor chores.

"You can't go on like this, child," Scott said one morning when she came in with a load of firewood that some men would hesitate to carry.

"It's alright. Evaleen come over yesterday and helped me a lot. You didn't notice your bed was clean?" For an instant she had felt like teasing but it didn't seem right. She sat down beside him at the table. "Do you think she's going to get better, Daddy?"

He shook his head and she took that to mean that he didn't and started to cry. He reached for her hand and held it tightly in both of his. "Honey, I just meant that I'm confused. The doctors are saying two different things and her family is saying we should never have let 'em do the surgery till she was built up better." He rose and went to the window, looking out over the yard and fields, remembering all the work he and Lillian had put into the place. Of course, he hadn't been able to do the hard jobs but with his sons and brothers helping, they had managed. But what if that's what's killing her? All that work and without her, it would mean nothing. "I hate this holler," he said and it was a minute or two before he realized he had spoken aloud.

"It's the only home …."

"I know that!" Scott yelled harshly, "but it won't be home without her. Will it?"

Metha didn't answer. She ran out into the stifling mid-day air and began to gather more firewood. This is stupid - having a fire in the middle of summer! "Jack!" she yelled, just as harshly as her father had. "Get out here and help me. Now!"

Toward the middle of June, Lillian began having life-threatening hemorrhages and was encouraged to go to the hospital. "Alright, if it happens again, I'll go," she agreed.

It was early one morning in July that Scott called, "Metha, get in here and help me. Your Mama's hemorrhaging. It's bad this time, girl." He was struggling to breathe as he hurried to get dressed by the dim light of the kerosene lamp. "Hurry, Metha, hurry," was all he could think to say.

Hours later, the doctors and nurses at Harriman Hospital had done all they could. There was no more hope outside a miracle. Lillian lay with her eyes closed, her breathing shallow. Reaching for Scott's hand she made every effort to sit up but it wasn't going to happen. "The children, the children," she seemed to choke on each word but refused to give up. "Tell the children …."

"They'll all be here in a few minutes, Lil. You just rest."

Metha had mopped up the bedroom floor as best she could and asked Uncle Dewey to help her carry the mattress and bedclothes out to the back yard, out of sight. She quickly wrote a note to leave on the table for anyone who stopped by. With all that, she had not had time to change her clothes, but no one seemed to notice.

Now, in the tiny hospital room, she leaned over the bed and touched her mother's face. "I'm here, Mama, I'm right here. Jack and Cally are here, too." She had awakened the kids before they left home but led them into the bedroom in a way that they couldn't see what was happening. Now they were just seeing Mama sleeping.

Scott sat down on the other side of the bed and lifted Lillian into his arms. "Oh, my love. My life. Don't leave me." His tears splashed onto her lovely face as he rocked back and forth the way one might do to quiet a baby, but she was already quiet.

Suddenly the door swung open and Junior and Polke rushed in, their agonized cries resounding around the room. Scott stood and moved to the other side of the room, motioning for Cally to come to him. Jack stood at the foot of the bed, silent tears streaming down his adorable little face.

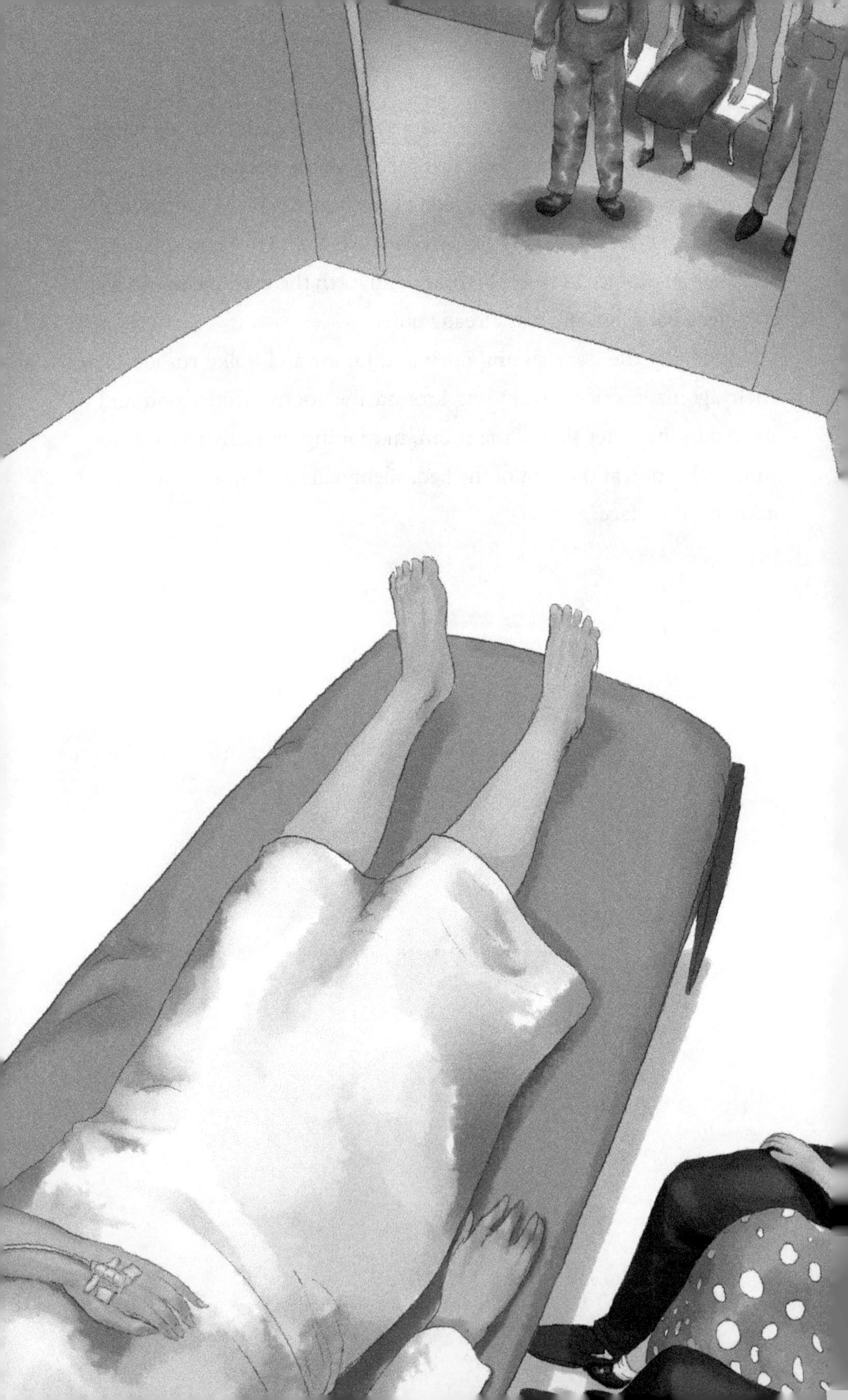

If you looked through the open door, and across the hall, you would see Evaleen, beloved daughter-in-law, crying softly into Bonnie June's colorful flour-sack dress that her Granny Wiggins had made for her. Mabel, also a beloved daughter-in-law, stood stiff and erect beside her, trying desperately not to cry. And a little further down would be a forever friend, Corine Whitaker Harris Monroe, sobbing pitifully into a tattered handkerchief.

Looking a little to the left, you would see Lillian's family, with memories flooding their very souls, back to a better, more precious time of growing up together. From Evan, the oldest, to Vernal, affectionately known as Kern, the baby. Evan was stoic in an effort to hold in his tears, his wife, Grace holding on to his arm, but Dewey cried as though his heart would break, remembering all the good times and still grieving over those loved ones they had lost. His wife, Hazel, kept slipping him dainty little hankies that did no good.

Jennie's husband, Sam, had hurriedly slipped a chair into place just in time for her to collapse. Joe and Gladys, the "almost twins" held hands as they leaned against the cold wall, with Joe's wife, Marie, encircled in his other arm. Kern practically wore a path in the hospital floor, pacing in his nervousness. They were all ready to scream at him, so his wife, Bill, tried to convince him to go downstairs with her to watch all the children. It was no use, none of them would leave for a long, long time.

Time stood still for all those who waited; the loneliness and heartache already swallowing them up in a dark cloud. There had been no movement or sound from Lillian for several hours. Suddenly, like her mother before her, she roused with a moment of clarity and reassurance.

One word escaped her parched lips. "Family."

Scott hurried to reassure her they were all there. A brief smile lit up her eyes, then she turned to her beloved husband. "Don't cry, Scott," she whispered, "you gave me everything I ever wanted. I am so grateful." She swallowed hard and continued. "Junior. Junior, look at me, son. I couldn't have loved you any more than I did. Impossible. And Polke, you were my special boy." Her voice gave out again and tears flowed from the corners of her eyes, soaking the pillow.

"Metha," there, her beautiful voice once more. "My special girl. I stopped dipping that nasty snuff. The Lord helped me. I know you prayed for me and I thank you!"

Metha dropped to her knees on the hard tile floor. "Then that makes it right, Mama. That makes it right." Tears of gratitude to the Lord and for her mother's courage filled her eyes. She reached for Jack and Cally, pulling them close so Lillian could see them.

Making one last heroic effort, Lillian cried out, "Jack, you were the light of my life, Little Boy!"

And then the voice was silent forevermore.

So much had fallen on Metha's shoulders and still she had the funeral arrangements to help make, had to try and keep the house clean and make sure everyone would have decent clothes to wear to the services. Now she had to search for her sister.

All morning church and community members had been coming and going with food and condolences and somewhere in the crowd, Cally had heard the question, "What's going to happen to that poor little girl?" She had run from the room in tears and found a hiding place so quickly that Metha was at a loss. She had poked her head into all the known cubby holes around the yard and still no Cally. She was just ready to give up and ask for help when she noticed the slightest movement above her head. Looking up she got a face full of pine needles. "Glenneva Wiggins! Get down out of that tree. You scared me to death, thinking of all the things that could have happened to you!" Cally dropped lightly to the ground and Metha's voice softened when she saw the tear-stained face. They sat side by side under the tree, Metha pretending she had all the time in the world.

Finally, Cally stirred. "What's going to happen to me?" she asked so quietly that Metha had to lean down to hear her.

"Honey, nothing is going to happen to you. What makes you ask that?"

"No, I mean Mama's dead, and Daddy's sick and you're going away." Tears streamed down her face as she tried to explain. "I don't want to live here with just all boys."

It would have been comical if it weren't so heartbreaking. "Baby, listen to me. I'm not going anywhere so we'll be two girls here together."

"Nuh uh. You'll go back to that school and forget all about me."

"Didn't you hear me? I'm not going anywhere." Metha emphasized each word so there would be no doubt in the little girl's heart. "How long have you known me?"

Cally managed a grin. "I'm eight years old – is that it?"

"Yes, and in all those years, have I ever told you something that wasn't true?"

A shake of the head.

"Have I ever made you do something you didn't want to do?"

Another shake of the head then a giggle. "You made me come down out of the pine tree!"

They laid their beloved Lillian Burse Adcock Wiggins to rest in the Estes Cemetery in Coalfield. Gone was the daughter, the wife, the mother, the granny, the sister, the aunt – on and on the circle went, drawing them in to emptiness and heartache but hope for the future. See you in the morning, Granny.